Call Me Den Mother

By Ryan Maitland

Preface

So, my editor got tired of me complaining about stopping the story to give you readers the necessary information to fully understand what's going on with these books, so he suggested I get as much of the exposition as possible out of the way right at the beginning, so here goes…

My name is Jane Allison Doe and I am writing these memoirs from the year 2086 in an effort to dispel some of the hero-worshipping I've seen about my life and to clear up some misunderstandings and outright lies that have been put out there.

Because of the nature of my life, namely my classified work with the CIA, FBI, and one or two others, most of the names you see in this book are fictitious. The only two names that are real are mine, Jane Doe, and that of Mr. Fluffybutt. All other names are ones I have adopted for the people in my life. Some of the names are flattering, others will tell you something about that person, while others are my personal jabs at people I distinctly dislike. Some of the names are even fairly neutral, generic, names, for people that I didn't really care about one way or another.

Most of the places I mention aren't the real places, either. Giving a fake name to a city would be odd, at best, and deranged at worst. I'll usually pick a city name that's close to where the events actually took place, but I might also pick a city with the same feel that isn't so close.

So, as far as names go, you have been warned. Almost all names in these books have some sort of meaning.

Since we're here, I might as well mention something about the book you're about to read. This particular part of my story took place immediately after I got back from the events of Call Me Acolyte. I've been hesitant to write about this part of my life, because it's one of those events that have been aggrandized to the point of absurdity. It also highlights one of the more stressful times of my life, since it deals with misinformation, Russian agents, and how hopeless I am around people.

In short, this story is embarrassing to me, but it's also an important part of my history.

And so, with that, here we go…

Chapter 1

Emily Pathos

Stupid vegetarian psychic…

Earl has saddled me with an annoying psychic housemate and I hate it!

Okay, I should probably back up a bit here. It's only been a few days since Earl brought me back home from the hospital after getting shot in the leg. At this point, my left leg is still in a cast, I walk around on crutches, and I'm always tired or hungry. I spend almost all my time on the first floor of my home, since going up or down stairs with crutches is agonizingly slow and frustrating. The only times I go upstairs at this point is to go to bed or take the additional small flight of stairs up to my serenity room, which I've been limiting to once a day out of necessity. Truth be told, I find it hard to get to sleep without a visit to the little room that used to be a nursery. Like the name implies, it's a room of peace and comfort, and it always stills my racing mind.

My house has been described as a mini-mansion in the Victorian style. It was built at a time when every room had a specific function, from receiving people, to the gathering room, the dining room, the library, and I'm pretty sure one of the rooms would have been called the smoking room, based on the lingering smell I've never been able to get out. The outside of the house is what most people would call the epitome of a haunted house, from the old gravel driveway, to the large stone and iron fence surrounding the property, to the large windows, and the parapet that holds the serenity room overlooking the little estate. The house is old and was built by one of the richest families at the time, but it was abandoned after tragedy hit in the form of the mother and father losing their two children after a freak snowstorm interrupted their game of hide-and-seek. The younger son, Peter, stayed out longer than he should have trying to find his older sister, Wendy, and ended up getting pneumonia and dying a few days later. Wendy, meanwhile, had become hopelessly lost in the woods and froze to death before anyone found her body.

I know all this because my house has a reputation for being haunted by the ghosts of these two children and stories get around quickly in a small town. To be fair, though, the house really *is* haunted by Peter and Wendy, but I try to dissuade people from believing this, since I already have a reputation of my own for being pretty creepy and maybe a witch.

Which brings us to this scene…

"Earl is here!" Wendy called, flying into the living room where I was napping on the couch.

"And there's someone behind him!" Peter added, grinning from ear to ear, mischief twinkling in his eyes.

The two kids looked the same age as each other, though I knew Wendy was several years older. Both were dressed in what is, for them, casual dress, with Wendy wearing an ankle-length dress and Peter in tan slacks and a dark blue shirt with red suspenders. The kids are the only ghosts I've ever met that actually fly, rather than pretend they can stand on the ground. I think part of the reason for this is because both of them are big fans of a children's book featuring a flying boy that never grows old, and partly because kids have an easier time in believing in the impossible.

For a ghost, believing is being, so they can appear any age they like, wearing whatever they want, and doing what they want just by believing they can. In this case, the kids believe they can fly, and so they do!

I sat up groggily, disturbing Max the manx, who had been napping quite comfortably on my chest. Max is a large black-and-white cat with long hair and no tail. He looks like a black cat with white markings that are somewhat reminiscent of a skeleton. He responds to Peter and Wendy, and even plays with them from time to time, though I'm not sure if *all* cats can see ghosts, or if it's just him.

Max let his irritation at being disturbed be known by giving a mournful yowl before sauntering up the stairs to the second floor, where he was less likely to be disturbed, at least by me, the little coward.

I sat there, rubbing my eyes, while trying to make sense of what the kids were telling me. Something about Earl and… somebody?

I glanced about for a clock to give me an idea of the time, but didn't see one at hand. Gotta fix that eventually, I thought to myself. I leaned over to a nearby table and grabbed my phone, which showed it was after three, and judging by how bright it was outside, my money was on it being in the afternoon.

I reached down to the crutches I've had to rely on, which were laying on the floor ready to trip anyone that dared get too close to me, and hobbled to the entry-room which bridged the living room and the dining room to the outside world. The room was spacious enough for several people to stand around talking, but little else. I glanced outside to see Earl's dark sedan with tinted windows that practically *screamed* government agent. Behind his car was a smaller one that made me think of a clown car, it was so tiny. The car was white and had a stubby hood and looked to be a hatchback of some kind. I've never been allowed to drive, due to my medical condition, so I'm not as familiar with the different species of car out there, but this one looked like it was built with practicality in mind, rather than muscle; a gas-sipper, rather than a gas-guzzler.

I recognized Earl with his dark suit, tie, fedora, and lopsided goatee. The woman getting out of the car behind him, though, was new to me. She looked to be taller than I was, which isn't really saying much since I'm five-foot-nothing, even with heavy boots on. She had dark black hair, cut boyishly short, and large blue eyes that would not look out-of-place in an anime. Her round, babyish, face gave the impression of youth, but her clothes, which looked like they had become vintage only *after* she had bought them, belied this belief.

The part that worried me most about this woman, though, was the fact that she was carrying suitcases, one in each hand, along with a shoulder bag. This did not bode well…

"Hi Earl!" I called to him cheerfully, hiding my dread at what I suspected was about to happen. "Who's your friend?" I added, tension rising in my voice.

"Jane," he smiled, looking like he was looking forward to what was about to happen, which was another sign this would not go well for me, "this is Emily Pathos. Emily, this is Jane Doe. The two of you will be living together for a while."

"Excuse me?" I seethed. "What was that?"

"Could we, maybe, take this *inside?"* the woman, Emily, asked, looking nervous.

"Fine," I groaned, giving up for the moment, but *only* for the moment. I planned to fight Earl on this if I had to. If he was doing to saddle me with *another* live-in nurse, I would give him hell!

I ushered the two of them into the dining room, since it was big enough for everyone to sit down and discuss matters without having to crane our necks to look at each other.

The dining room is my third-favorite room in the house, after the serenity room and kitchen. The room looks like it was built around a huge table that can sit ten people comfortably, without anyone bumping elbows, with space around the edges for servants to serve meals without bumping into the back of anyone's chair. The table, itself, is large and made of hardwood. It's so large, in fact, that I'm pretty sure the table was here before the room was, as moving it anywhere, now, would entail knocking out a wall or two.

I sat at the head of the table, closest to the door to the kitchen, but Earl and Emily seemed to prefer standing around, with Earl leaning against a wall and Emily looking decidedly uncomfortable with her two suitcases of luggage.

I confess I wasn't really doing anything to alleviate her discomfort, but in my defense, I don't typically do well with people, much less people invading my home.

"Okay, Earl, *talk!*" I demanded, glaring at him. "Who is she, what's she doing here, and why does she have suitcases?"

I saw the woman take a deep, calming, breath right before I felt a swarm of ants running across my scalp.

"STOP THAT!" I screamed at her, furiously.

"Stop what?" she asked, looking utterly dumfounded.

"Whatever the hell it is you're *doing!*" I growled at her. "Look, I take it you're a strong broadcaster, but whatever it is you *think* you're doing, *stop it!* It's not working and it's seriously pissing me off!"

"Emily…" Earl warned quietly.

"Okay, okay!" she relented, holding her hands up as the ants disappeared from my hair. "But, how did you know I was doing anything?"

"Because it felt like I had *bugs* sprinting across my *head!*" I almost shrieked, panting a little. Dammit, I must be the only person on the *planet* that gets a cardio workout just from getting angry!

"What? How?" she spluttered, looking more than a little terrified.

"Emily, meet Jane Doe," Earl reintroduced. "Jane is a strong sensitive *and* a strong broadcaster and seems to be immune to the effects of *other* strong broadcasters, including you, it seems."

"Jane," Earl continued, turning to me, "this is Emily Pathos, an emmy, as in, she can alter the emotions of those around her, like a reverse empath."

"Wait!" Emily demanded, "I'm still confused. You say you could *feel* what I was trying to do, even though I was just trying to calm you down?"

I took a few moments to catch my breath before answering. "Yes, I could feel it, but it wasn't as bad as Bishop, at least."

"Bishop?" she asked, looking utterly confused.

"Randall Bishop," Earl answered. "He was a strong cultist that Jane encountered on her last job."

"Is that why your leg is in a cast?" she asked, glancing down.

"More or less," I sighed, wishing I had my scratching pole as part of my leg was getting itchy. Stupid cast. "I got shot by a brainwashed cop while fleeing his sex cult," I added, glancing around to see if I had left it in the dining room, or if it was still by the couch in the living room. Pretty sure it was still by the couch… dammit!

Emily glanced at Earl, her face a mask of worry, "Is she kidding?"

"Nope!" Earl smirked, seeming to enjoy watching her squirm.

"Stupid jackass cop," I muttered more or less under my breath.

"Wait!" Emily demanded. "Are you saying you got shot by a *cop?*"

"Well, he's not a cop anymore," Earl almost purred, "but he was at the time."

"Now, can you *please* tell me why she's here?" I demanded of Earl.

"Emily is between jobs at the moment and needs a safe place to stay," Earl explained.

"Okay, so why *here?*" I huffed.

"Call it a test!" Earl smirked.

"A test for whom?" I glared at the man.

At that, Earl's evil smirk only grew in intensity.

"Dammit Earl!" I screamed at him.

"Look, she needs a place to stay for a while and I know you've got a spare room, or two, that you're not using, so why not let her stay here?" Earl placated.

"Just how long is 'a while'?" I asked, *certain* I wouldn't like the answer.

"Not sure," he shrugged. "Could be days, weeks, or maybe a month!"

"A *month?*" I gasped.

"Maybe two," he added, unhelpfully.

"Earl…" I growled in warning.

"Did I mention that the agency will be paying you for room and board?" Earl grinned, like he was finally done playing whatever evil prank he had been pulling.

"How much?" I asked more eagerly than I would have liked. The antique store wasn't doing so well and I was having to rely more and more on the jobs Earl gave me to make ends meet, so any extra source of income was welcomed, even if I didn't like the one providing it.

"A thousand dollars should cover her first month," Earl answered, pulling out a check and handing it to me. I studied it carefully, seeing that Earl had used the alias Max Flagg as the one paying the money.

"Fine," I surrendered with a sigh. "You can have one of the rooms upstairs except the master bedroom or the serenity room. Consider those two rooms off-limits to you, but the kids will probably keep you out of them, anyway."

I glanced at Peter and Wendy, who were floating between me and the two guests. Peter was floating partway through the table, while Wendy was a little off to the side. Both nodded understanding before flying off to close the doors in question, which both slammed shut with a loud *bang* a second, or so, later, making both Emily and Earl jump. Emily even gave out a little shriek that I confess I enjoyed a little more than I probably should have!

"You have kids?" she asked, her voice sounding like she hadn't fully recovered from her shock at the loud noises.

"Sort-of," I shrugged. "They're ghosts," I added, watching her face carefully.

At this, Emily rolled her eyes like I was speaking utter nonsense.

"She's right," Earl warned the woman. "Peter and Wendy are not to be taken lightly."

"Wait," she demanded, shaking her head in disbelief, or maybe terror, "are you saying that ghosts are *real?*"

"'Fraid so," I sighed, knowing what was coming next and wishing I had thought to bring a sweatshirt or something.

"You're joking, right? Hazing the new girl?" she questioned, somewhat frantically. "I mean, ghosts aren't *real!*"

And there it was.

Peter and Wendy were *furious!* They started screaming, bringing a little whirlwind to the dining room while the temperature fell at an alarming rate. I hugged myself tighter and started shivering as the chairs started rattling, threatening to rise up and fly through the air.

"Kids!" I screamed at them, *"Enough!"*

"She started it..." Peter whined.

"I know she started it," I sighed, feeling like an overworked mother, "but she just doesn't know the rules yet, okay?"

Peter and Wendy were looking forlorn, Emily looked positively terrified, while Earl was just smirking, looking like he was having to hold back a loud guffaw.

"What just happened?" Emily gasped, wide-eyed.

"For the record," I intoned, "ghosts *hate* it when you say they're not real. They take it personally, since your believing that *makes* them less real. It literally *hurts* them when you say shit like that, okay?"

"Um..." Emily mumbled, looking totally unsure of what was going on.

"Okay, short-version," I sighed, seeing that I would have to give a lecture. "Ghosts are real. This house really *is* haunted by two kids that died over a century ago, but the good news is that I'm on good terms with them. Ghosts follow a number of rules that I can tell you about later, but one of those is that belief makes them stronger and the fact that I can see, hear, and feel them has made Peter and Wendy among the strongest ghosts I've ever encountered."

"Oh," Emily squeaked, looking like she was ready to bolt out the door, leaving her luggage behind in favor of adding more speed to her sprint.

Too bad Earl was between her and the door… which I'm *sure* wasn't an accident…

"Look," I added, "They know to give you your privacy, so the bathrooms and bedrooms are off-limits to them when people are there, so don't worry about that, okay?"

"Um, okay, I guess…" she mumbled, looking around the room like she was looking for the kids, or maybe another way out.

"Now, I thought you were with Project Aesop and so knew that ghosts were real…" I lamented.

"Why would I think that?" she asked, looking pissed.

"Well, for one thing," I huffed, "I caught two serial-killers that used ghosts, and people sensitive to ghosts are common enough that there's a slang word for them."

Emily looked to Earl with a face that practically *begged* him to tell her that I was kidding.

"Not kidding," Earl answered her unasked question. "Frankly, her being a spooky is more of a hindrance than anything else. It means we can't do our work here, since the kids interfere with the electronics."

"So, you expect me to live in a *literal* haunted house?" she whined.

"Think of the ghosts as extra security, like guard dogs!" Earl snorted.

At this, Wendy flicked Earl's hat off his head, throwing it to Peter, who promptly chucked it out the front door.

Earl growled after the retreating hat before giving chase.

"Guess the kids didn't like being called dogs," I mumbled around a yawn. Now that things had quieted down, albeit only a little, my body had started relaxing enough that it felt comfortable telling me that the nap I had been taking before all this started hadn't been *nearly* enough for its liking!

Earl finally came back into the dining room, amidst giggles from the kids, and huffed, "Okay, before I leave, Emily, I want you to consider Jane to be the senior agent here."

"What?" Emily gasped. "How long has this girl been an agent?"

"A few years now," Earl shrugged.

"Well, I've been an agent for more than a *decade!*" she growled. "Plus! I'm *older* than she is!"

"True, but Jane is more mature," Earl smirked. Many have come to hate that smirk and for good reason.

"What do you *mean* she's more *mature?*" she whined.

"Do you *really* want me to give you the reasons?" Earl quipped.

"Name *one!*" she demanded.

"Well, didn't your parents just kick you out of the house?" Earl asked, obviously leading her into a trap.

"So?" Emily responded, taking the bait.

"Well, Jane, here, *owns* this house and has owned it for *longer than I've known her!"* Earl gleefully sprang the trap.

"Oh, so you mean that the agency paid for her house?" Emily countered, with a look that told me she thought she had won.

"Um, no," I remarked quietly. "I paid for this house on my own, from a grant…"

"Wait, *seriously?*" she asked, sounding perplexed.

"Well… yeah…" I responded, not really knowing why she was having so much trouble believing this.

"Oh, then you must have had rich parents!" she relented.

"Nope!" Earl smiled, clearly enjoying this.

"Look," I sighed, hating to have to go into my personal life so soon after meeting her, "I ran away from home when I was fourteen, managed to get a grant from a source I am not at liberty to tell you about, but just know that I damned well *earned* that money. At that point, I was adopted by a woman and I spent a few years with her, before moving out here, buying this house, and using the money I saved to fix it up to livable levels."

"What do you mean by 'money you saved'?" she asked, looking like she was having a hard time believing *any* of what I was saying.

"Peter tended to chase away anyone buying the house," I shrugged. "I was the first one to last more than a week in the house. It was getting to the point that nobody would even consider the house, so I got it much cheaper than I would have otherwise!"

"This is insane…" she muttered, under her breath…

"Anyway," Earl announced loudly, trying to bring back our focus to the matter at hand, "Jane is to be the senior agent because she's been an adult for longer than you have!"

"What? How?" Emily gasped. "Earl, I'm *older* than she is, so by *definition* I've been an adult longer than she has!"

"Pfft!" I snorted, rolling my eyes at her. At this point I was beginning to see Earl's point.

"Okay, just why do you think *you've* been an adult longer than I have?" she demanded.

"Crappy childhood," I answered, somewhat smugly.

"What do you mean?" she asked.

"Take my word for it," Earl warned. "She's practically been an adult all her life. Be nice and let her take the lead, okay? Besides, this is her house, and you're the guest, after all, okay?"

"Alright, fine!" Emily relented, looking displeased.

Right after that, Earl beat a hasty retreat and Emily lugged her suitcases upstairs looking for a room.

I was lecturing the kids to be nice to her while she stayed here, and having to negotiate a trade of no less than *three* bedtime stories a night when Emily made her presence known, clearing her throat.

I took a moment to imagine how it must have looked to her, with me talking about reading bedtime stories to the middle of the table, where nothing sat, and lamented how utterly abnormal my life was.

"Are you sure you're not, like…" she hesitated, probably looking for a nice way of saying what she wanted, "that you're not crazy?" she winced, knowing it was probably the wrong thing to say.

"I am, but not *that* way," I sighed, feeling too tired to fight her, at this point.

"What do you mean?" she asked, the look of confusion looking more and more at home on her face since she got here.

"PTSD" I answered, curtly.

"I'm just going to assume you're not kidding…" she muttered, sounding somewhat exasperated.

"Good call," I agreed.

"So, um… what's for dinner?" she asked, her voice sounding somewhat hopeful.

"I was thinking steaks," I answered, a smile coming to my face at the thought of them cooking.

"Um… steaks are evil…" she almost whined uncomfortably.

"Say what?" I mumbled, not sure I heard her correctly.

"Meat is murder," she asserted confidently.

"No, *murder* is murder…" I huffed. "Meat is just… *meat!*"

Emily was starting to look *much* more uncomfortable at that moment.

"Aw, hell and blast!" I gasped, realization coming to me. "Don't tell me! You're a… *vegetarian!*"

"Damn straight!" she smiled.

That's it! I'm in hell! No other way to put it! Earl had sent a freaking *vegetarian* to me and expected me to feed her! I might have to make… *salads!*

EUGH!

Shoot me now…

Chapter 2

Shopping Trip from Hell

"I don't have any vegetarian options here," I insisted to Emily, for what felt like the hundredth time.

"Come *on!*" she insisted right back. "You must have *something!* Nobody can eat *just* meat!"

"The closest things I have to non-meat are…" I paused, doing a mental inventory of what I had in the fridge and pantry, "potatoes and mushrooms."

"I…" Emily hesitated, probably doing some kind of mental rundown of the things she could prepare with those, "I might be able to make those work, like a baked potato and some sautéed mushrooms, but… you seriously don't have *any* vegetables here?"

"Not really," I shrugged. "Look, we can go to the store and you can buy what you want, just understand that I refuse to take part in your twisted dietary restrictions!"

"What have you got against salads?" she asked, sounding suspicious.

"Crappy childhood," I waved off, dismissively.

"That involved *salads?*" she countered in disbelief.

"*Yes*," I insisted. "Look, if you *must* know, picture this: starving girl with a medical condition that practically demands more protein than normal being forced to eat plain salad, no dressing, croutons, cheese, or meat of any kind, just raw vegetables, while her father cooks up actual *meat* right in *front* of her, where she can freaking *smell* the deliciousness that is being denied her, because if she were to, heaven forbid, ask to have some of that meat, she'd be whipped with a bamboo switch within an inch of her *life!*"

By this time, I was panting bad enough that I worried I would pass out. Dammit, I *really* need to stop getting so upset with her… at least until I had recovered a bit more.

"I think you're probably exaggerating…" she considered, quietly, "but I'm willing to give you the benefit of the doubt," she placated quickly, probably after seeing me glare at her menacingly.

"How about this," I proposed, "we head to the store, you can pick what you want, then we'll come back, and I can prepare a baked potato, some mushrooms sautéed in butter, then cook up some meat for me and Max, then we can eat in peace, okay?"

"Who's Max?" she asked, sounding curious and a little fearful.

"He's my cat," I answered, "or I'm his human, depending on how you look at it."

She nodded acquiescence and pulled out her keys. "Shall I drive?" she asked.

"You'll have to," I sighed. "I'm not allowed to drive."

"Because of the leg," she assumed.

"Because of my blood," I shot back. Before she could ask, I answered, "Anemia that sometimes makes me pass out if I work too hard. I use a bike to get where I need to go in town, and beg for a ride when I need to go out of town."

She seemed to accept that and left out the front door, with me following her.

"I'll be back in a little bit!" I called to the kids before locking the door behind me.

Her car looked to be a rental, judging by the sticker on the windshield, and was smaller than I had first thought. I got in awkwardly, having to hop on one leg as I maneuvered myself into the seat, placing the crutches between my legs. Emily looked like she was trying to be patient while also holding back any offer to help. To be fair, if she had offered to help me, I'm pretty sure I would have growled at her. I prize my independence, which was why I insisted on getting around town on my bike, rather than always bothering people for a ride.

We got underway and I directed her to the local grocery store. She grabbed a cart and went straight for the produce section, while I lagged a little behind on my crutches. I was beginning to wonder whether I should have just stayed in the car when I saw someone wearing a bright red, color-coordinated, outfit heading straight for me. The woman looked to be in her late forties and was on the petite, but somewhat plump, side.

She's also one of the banes of my existence…

Aw, hell and blast! I did *not* need this now!

"Whatever happens, follow my lead," I warned Emily, who did not see the danger that was heading straight for us.

"Jane!" Beth, the realtor, called to me. "Where have you *been?* What happened to your leg? Who is your friend? Oh, I missed seeing you! Why haven't you called?" she asked, shotgunning the questions in rapid fire.

"I fell down some stairs while visiting relatives," I lied, using the story Earl had come up with and that Sarah, my foster mother, would back if called upon.

"Oh, I'm so sorry to hear that!" Beth lamented. "But it looks like you made a new friend!"

"Yes, this is Emily, a friend from out of town," I agreed, unable to come up with a more detailed lie. Honestly, the more detail you throw into a lie, the more likely it is to fall apart, anyway, so it's best to keep it vague and let others fill in the holes themselves.

"How do you do?" Emily greeted, holding out her hand to the woman.

"I'm doing well, thank you for asking!" Beth cooed with a cheerful smile. I could already see the gears in her head working overtime, reading more into it than there was.

"Emily had a sort-of falling out with her family," I threw in, earning me a glare from the woman in question, "so I offered her a spare room while she works things out."

I saw a brief look of suspicion cross Beth's face, only to be replaced with one of total belief. The fact that this change in her demeanor was accompanied by an aggressive army of ants marching across my scalp did *not* escape my attention, though I fought hard not to show this on my own face.

"Oh, that can be rough," Beth soothed, sympathetically. "These are certainly difficult times for everyone and tempers can get heated."

"They sure can!" Emily agreed, spearing me with a glance that I pretended not to notice.

The two talked for a bit more, with Beth asking probing questions while Emily answered noncommittally, giving only the vaguest of the vague responses. She managed to get away with this because she was constantly broadcasting whatever emotional signal Beth was picking up, while I had to keep a death-grip on my crutches to keep from scratching my head bloody!

The encounter finally, *blessedly*, came to an end and Emily and I were once again left alone in the produce section.

"Who was that?" Emily asked over the heads of lettuce.

"That was Beth, the realtor and town gossip," I answered, sighing with relief now that my head felt bug-free. "Try to avoid her if you can."

"Did you *have* to tell her I had a falling-out with my parents?" she asked, irritation in her voice.

"Better that than whatever she was coming up with," I sighed. "She was probably about to tell people you're my lesbian lover or something…"

"Do you really think she'd do something like that?" she asked, sounding shocked.

"Maybe," I shrugged. "Wouldn't put it past her. She has a habit of constructing elaborate stories about people and I'm a frequent subject of hers."

"Why is that?" she wondered, seemingly to herself.

"I guess because I'm pretty odd," I lamented. "I mean, I bought my house when I was underage, paid it off in full, and live alone. She tried to hook me up on a date that went straight to hell, and has never understood why it didn't work out."

"Oh? So why *didn't* it work out?" she smirked, perhaps trying to picture me on a date and having a hard time of it.

"He ordered his steak *well-done* and then *smothered* it in *ketchup*!" I gave an involuntary shudder and let out a sound of disgust, wincing at the memory.

"That can't be the *only* reason it didn't work out, though!" Emily chided.

"Not the only reason," I agreed, "but that, alone, was enough! At least for me!"

Emily scowled at this, though I'm not sure why. Maybe she thought that all levels of done-ness were the same when it came to steak, or maybe she didn't see the problem with using ketchup on a steak.

Honestly? Who knows with her? I was having a hard time figuring the woman out. From what I could tell, her life must have been pretty easy, since she could use her ability to soothe any frayed tempers and get her own way. The fact that she was a decade older than me, yet was still living with her parents, at least until recently, was abhorrent to me, since I value my privacy so much.

And I won't even start on her dietary choices… Ugh! Freaking *salads!*

We managed to finish in the produce section and were making our way to an aisle that promised salad dressing when a tall, lanky, man in a light blue shirt and faded jeans walked up to me and I had to suppress a stream of profanities at the universe for doing this to me.

Honestly? This is what I get for *not* checking the app Earl gave me to track Tim's whereabouts. Mind you, the tracking app is probably illegal, but I don't question it too much, since it's so handy to have.

At least when I remember to check it…

"Jane?" came his boyish voice a moment later.

"Tim! Hi!" I cheered to the best of my abilities. "Didn't think I'd see you here!"

"Yeah, they've got me running a story here about…" he continued, though at this point I was largely tuning him out as I plotted my escape.

"Jane, who is your friend here?" Emily admonished gently.

Aw, hell and blast! I kinda forgot she was here!

"Emily, this is Tim Foyle," I introduced. "He's a journalist at the local paper. Tim, this is Emily Pathos. She's a friend from out of town that's staying with me."

"Minor fight with my parents," Emily added, shaking Tim's hand, obviously going with the story I had crafted earlier. Always good to keep lies consistent.

"So, what happened to your leg?" Tim asked, pointing to my leg.

"I fell down some stairs while visiting relatives," I answered more on automatic at this point. I confess that the lie was cliché, but those exist because they *work!*

"Oh, I'm sorry to hear that," he consoled, looking suspicious.

Emily must have noticed this as I felt the ants on my scalp soon afterwards.

Oh, she and I would have to have a talk about that later, but for now, suppressing Tim's suspicions were of *paramount* importance.

"I've always wondered about your relatives," Tim mused aloud.

"Just a foster-mother and a couple of her kids," I answered slowly, wondering just how much I was comfortable telling him.

"Do you know who your real family is?" he asked, sounding like a journalist looking for a story.

"Not really," I lied, trying to wave it away. "I figure if they gave me up, then why shouldn't I give up on them?"

Tim looked suspicious once more, telling me this was probably the *wrong* thing to say in that situation. Emily laid her power thickly, which seemed to ease his doubts, at least for a while. When his face turned suspicious once again, despite the ants on my scalp, I touched Emily's arm and opened up my other sense.

'Stop using your ability,' I warned her, sending my thoughts directly into her head without the need to speak out loud. *'He's getting suspicious of it,'* I added for good measure.

Emily jumped a little at this, but relented as I felt the bugs go away.

"I'm sorry to hear that," Tim eventually told us. "Maybe I could look into it for you?"

"I'd really rather you didn't," I confessed to him, earning me even more suspicion.

Dammit, what the hell was I supposed to do? If I told him to look into it, he probably *would,* and if I told him *not* to look into it, he'd *definitely* do it!

"Look, Tim," I sighed, touching him on the arm lightly, opening myself up again. "The truth is that I know who my blood relations are, and I wish I had never found out. They're some truly *awful* people, you know?"

As I was speaking out loud to him, I was whispering into his head, *'She looks so sad, like this is hurting her! She has a right to her privacy. Maybe I should let this go.'*

I was hoping that I was whispering soft enough that he'd hear them as his own thoughts and so agree to them. I got feelings of suspicion and of anticipation at being able to dig into my mysterious past, which panicked me for a moment, but then Emily pushed through a feeling of resignation that pushed him over the edge into agreeing with me.

Whew! That was *way* too damned close!

"So, do you think you'll be returning to the antique store soon?" he asked, seemingly out of nowhere, perhaps to change the topic.

"Eventually," I shrugged. "When I heal up a bit more. It's kind of awkward to get around as I am now, though…"

"Oh, I could help out at the store!" Emily chimed in, unhelpfully. "I've worked retail before!"

"I'll have to ask Anne," I chuckled, humorlessly, as I glared hate-daggers at her.

"I look forward to it, then!" Tim cheered, finally moving away from us, perhaps in response to the fact that I was starting to pant. I was feeling a little dead on my feet at this point. Using my ability like that, plus standing for so long, is difficult for me on my *best* days, let alone when I was recovering from a shattered leg bone…

Once Tim was out of sight, Emily turned on me with menace in her eyes as she asked, "Okay, what the *hell* was that?"

"That was Tim Foyle, journalist, conspiracy blogger, and overall pain in my ass," I answered with a sigh.

"No, not *that!*" she gruffed. "I meant you talking into my head!"

"Would you be *quiet?*" I hissed, looking around to see if anyone had overheard. "I'll tell you about that when we get *home!*"

Emily considered me a moment, but ultimately relented, probably rightly figuring that the information was classified.

"So, you gonna call up Anne and ask if I can help out?" she asked with a smile.

"Yeah, that's not gonna happen," I sighed. "You're not working there," I added, lest she get the wrong idea.

"Isn't that Anne's call?" she asked, sounding confused.

"Not really," I answered before quickly adding, "I'll tell you later."

"But," she started.

"Later!" I hissed, interrupting her.

Her face told me she was not satisfied with this answer, so I felt I had to give her *something* to assuage her enough to go with my decision to wait.

"Look," I started, trying to think of something I could tell her now that wouldn't compromise me. "Anne *runs* the store, but she doesn't *own* it, at least, not anymore."

"Really?" she asked, looking somewhat confused.

"Really," I sighed. "I'll tell you more once we get home," I repeated.

"But, back there with Tim," she insisted," were you reading his mind? Is that how you knew I should back off?"

"No," I lamented, seeing that she wasn't going to give this up without something more to chew on. "That was just me reading his face. No extra skill involved."

"Are you sure?" she asked, looking dubious.

"Totally," I answered, wondering why she *wasn't* so sure. "Look, I learned how to read people pretty damned well and I figured you had done the same, given who you work for!"

"Well, not *everyone* takes those elective classes!" she shot back.

"What classes?" I asked, befuddled at her response.

"But… you…" she stammered, utterly perplexed, "then *how?*" she demanded.

I gave her an 'are you serious' look before we *both* answered, "Crappy childhood."

We chuckled at this new inside joke before continuing the shopping.

The rest of the trip was amicable, and quiet, with Emily picking the dressing and toppings she wanted for her part of the meals while I followed her hoping we wouldn't run into anybody else I knew.

I confess I probably dozed on the way home. This little trip of ours had completely exhausted me.

Chapter 3

Jane's House

The next thing I remember clearly was Emily remarking, "I didn't know you had an automatic gate-opener!"

"I don't," I mumbled, only semi-coherent.

"Then how did…" she started, as her face took on a look of horror.

"The kids," I answered, anyway. "They watch out for me and they like flexing their powers, especially in ways I won't scold them for."

"You know what? I'm going to pretend it's an automatic gate-opener!" she declared, choosing denial over fact.

Whatever helps you through your day, I guess…

Emily parked in front of my house and grabbed her groceries, while I hobbled my way up the stairs, a step at a time, to the front door. The door opened before I could reach it and I saw Wendy's smiling face, floating at eye-level to me.

"Thank you, Wendy," I smiled, looking back to see Emily shaking her head, like she was trying to shake something loose inside.

"Welcome!" Wendy cheered before flying upstairs, with Peter right behind her. I saw them just outside the serenity room, looking eager. I smirked as I figured what they wanted.

"I'm gonna fix something for Max, and then you can make your own dinner," I called to Emily over my shoulder as I made my way inside.

"You're not eating?" Emily asked, sounding somewhat baffled.

"Not just now," I yawned. "Between all that walking, and using my ability like that, I'm in need of a nap."

"Won't you have trouble sleeping later, though?" she criticized.

"Probably not," I sighed, pulling out the bag of special raw food I bought online for Max. "I'm still recovering," I added as I saw her scornful look.

"I heard exercise is just what's needed to recover quickly!" she pouted. Why was she giving me such a hard time? Was it because she wanted me to cook for her or something?

"You heard wrong," I refuted as I scooped out a generous portion onto a small plate for the large cat.

"Max! Dinner!" I called, setting the plate on the table, just in front of the seat nearest the door, and opposite of where I usually sat to eat.

Max stealthily stalked into the room, saw Emily, and hissed at her!

"Max! Don't be rude!" I hissed back. "She's our guest!"

Max didn't look the least bit repentant as he jumped onto the seat, saw the plate of raw food, and seemed to look around for another plate.

"I'm too tired to make you something else," I sighed to the cat. "Look, I'll cook you something later, okay, but for now, this is what you're getting!"

Max glared at me, then looked to Emily, as if considering. Was he thinking of stalking her?

"Do you think he'd let me pet him?" Emily asked, looking eager.

"Probably not," I confessed. "He… doesn't really get on with people…"

I considered the cat a moment longer before realizing another quirk the cat has. Max has never started eating until I had sat down and was eating. It was one of a number of weird rules that he seems to have imposed on himself and me.

"You should probably make your food," I told Emily, edging towards the stairway. "Give Max his space and he'll probably start eating once you do. In the meantime, I'll be upstairs."

Emily looked uncertain, but nodded eventually.

I inched my way up the stairs, huffing a little, and finally made the second-floor landing. The kids were still hovering in front of the door that was just up another small flight of stairs. The door led to the room that used to be a small nursery, but was now my serenity room.

"Read us a story!" Wendy pleaded.

"Please?" Peter added, giving me his sad puppy-dog eyes.

"Oh, alright…" I smirked, knowing this was coming. Besides, it's not like I didn't get anything out of story-time.

The rocking chair in the room used to belong to their mother and was filled with emotions of motherly-love. I have ended up dozing in that chair more than a few times over the years I've lived in this house, and I'm thankful the kids don't seem to mind. I guess they see me as a surrogate mother-figure, though I never wanted to be.

So, I sat down in the beloved rocking chair and grabbed a tattered copy of the kids' favorite book and started reading to them, reveling in the emotions I picked up from the chair and the book.

"It's weird seeing you read to an empty room," Emily remarked, leaning in the doorway.

I wasn't the only one that had missed her coming up the stairs because Peter and Wendy both had faces full of shock. Peter even went so far as to slam the door in the poor girl's face!

"Peter!" I scolded harshly. "That was rude! Open the door for her!"

Peter sulked and opened the door slowly. Wendy looked mournful for her little brother, but the boy could have hurt Emily!

"What just happened?" Emily gasped, eyes wide.

"The kids are protective of this room," I explained. "So am I, for that matter…"

"Why?" she asked. "What's so special about this room?"

"It keeps me sane," I shrugged.

"Not following…" she admitted.

"Okay," I sighed, trying to gear myself up for a long explanation that I was feeling too tired to give. "How about if we explain our abilities to each other, since we're going to be living together?"

"Okay," she readily agreed.

"Okay," I echoed. "So, first of all, you know that I can see, hear, and feel ghosts, right?"

"Right," she agreed.

"But that's not the ability the CIA cares about," I added, eliciting a nod from her. "If I touch something," I continued, wearily, "and that object is emotionally significant to someone, then I can get into their heads."

"What do you mean, 'emotionally significant'?" she asked, sounding a little like a student.

"Something they care about," I answered, "or something they would miss," I added.

"Okay, so what do you mean by 'get into their heads' then?" she followed-up.

"I sense whatever they sense," I replied. "See what they see, hear what they hear, etcetera."

Emily nodded in understanding.

"If it's a good connection," I continued, "then I can hear their thoughts as well. From there, I can push further into their heads and talk to them."

"Like you did with me at the store," she mused.

"Exactly," I agreed. "If I speak softly enough into their heads, then they hear it as their internal monologue and they think they thought it up themselves."

"Sounds like brainwashing," she warned.

"Sometimes," I shrugged, "but I can only go so far before people realize it's not their voice they're hearing. Think gentle nudging, rather than dramatic shift."

"But you can speak louder than a whisper, since you did it to me, right?" she asked.

"Right," I agreed. "I don't typically do that, though, unless the person already knows about what I can do or if I can convince them that the voice belongs to an angel or devil or something."

"But, how does that ability relate to his room keeping you sane?" she wondered, looking around the room, but not daring to poke her head beyond the door-frame for fear of getting her face bashed in.

"Sometimes objects hold emotions," I explained, stroking the arm of the rocking chair fondly. "My ability lets me pick up on those emotions. The objects in this room have been carefully cultivated for the feelings they give me."

"That…" she hesitated, like she was choosing her words carefully, "sounds a little like drugs…"

I rolled my eyes at this before shaking my head. "Is it really any different than feeling happy when doing something fun?"

She looked like she thought about saying more before deciding to keep her mouth shut.

Probably a good idea.

"So, how about you?" I asked. "How does your ability work?"

"I can project my emotions onto others," she answered, a little automatically. I'm guessing she's had to explain this a few times in her life.

"Do you have to be experiencing those emotions?" I asked, a little interested.

"Yes," she replied shortly. "I've learned to control my emotions to the point that I can call up almost any of them with just a few moments of focus."

"What kind of range do you have?" I wondered, thinking back to the few times I've seen her use it.

"Only a few feet," she lamented. "And it affects everyone around me; I can't focus it on a single person."

"What does it feel like?" I asked.

"I…" she hesitated. "I can't really put it into words…"

"Okay, then let's try this," I suggested, holding out my hand. "Take my hand and try to alter my emotions."

Emily looked warily around the room, perhaps looking for Peter and Wendy, who were still sitting in front of me, albeit floating perhaps a foot off the floor.

"Kids, be nice!" I warned, more for Emily's sake than for theirs. "I think as long as you don't try to touch anything, they'll leave you alone, just this one time."

The kids nodded agreement, though Emily couldn't see them.

Emily visibly screwed up her courage, took a step inside, and gently grabbed my hand. I could feel her fear and got a sense that she *hated* ghost stories and now felt like she was *living* in one.

'Breathe' I told her through my link to her. *'Not all ghosts are bad. Most are just people trying to get by.'*

She steadied her breathing, then focused on creating joy by remembering a happy memory of a time when a boy she liked told her she looked cute. Once she had that memory firmly in place, I felt her push out, similar to how I push my senses out through my hands.

I ignored the wave of ants scurrying across my scalp and focused on how it felt to her to use her ability. I could feel an ephemeral bubble extending around her head and pushing outward in gentle pulses.

"Interesting," I remarked, somewhat idly. "Have you ever tried…" I fought for a good word to use to explain my idea, "to sort-of *squish* the bubble, so that it elongated, like right in front of you?"

"Not sure I…" she hesitated before reconsidering. "I've never thought about it that way…"

I could feel her picturing the bubble of emotions around her head. She imagined it as a sort of silvery, shimmering, fabric just beyond her eyes. I felt a surge of concentration, like she was pushing out with her eyes and I could feel the bubble shift, through her senses.

"Huh! I think that might work!" she proclaimed, feeling utterly surprised!

I let go of her hand, stifling a yawn, before asking, "Doesn't doing that make you tired?"

"Not really," she shrugged. "If I overuse it, I can get headaches, but I get a lot of warning beforehand. It feels like pressure building up, right behind my eyes. What about you?"

"If I'm just observing through a good connection," I sighed, feeling drowsy, "then I can maintain it for hours at a time, but I'd need a good long nap afterwards."

"Hours?" she gasped.

"When I have to," I remarked. "But talking to somebody, especially through a bad connection, wears me out really quickly."

"What about ghosts?" she asked, apparently satisfied with this aspect. "What's it like seeing ghosts?"

"They look like normal people to me," I answered around a yawn, "unless they're in their gory phase…"

"Gory phase?" she asked, her face blanching as she looked like she regretted asking me.

"When someone first dies," I explained, assuming a lecturing tone, "they don't always know that they're dead or that they follow different rules. They tend to look like how they died."

"Ew! Gross!" she proclaimed, making a face.

"You get used to it," I lied. The truth is that seeing some of the gory ghosts in cemeteries creep me the hell out and I'd rather avoid them if at all possible.

"You said they follow different rules," she followed-up. "What kind of rules?"

"Believing is being, is the main rule of ghosts," I answered. "If people believe in them, they become more real. When they believe they should look different, then they do."

"So, once they realize they don't *have* to look like zombies, then they *don't?"* she asked, though it was less of a question and more of a statement.

"Basically," I nodded. "Ghosts also can't move about freely."

"They can't?" she asked, looking shocked. "I thought the… *kids* moved all around the house!"

"They do," I explained. "Ghosts anchor to a person, place, or object that they can't move beyond. Peter and Wendy," I nodded towards the kids that Emily couldn't see, "are anchored to the house and the yard around it. Others are anchored to their own bodies, and some are anchored to the people they feel intense emotions about."

"How did you learn all this?" she asked, somewhat in disbelief.

"My first friend was a ghost," I answered, feeling a little embarrassed at this confession. "I didn't know he was a ghost when I first met him. Hell and blast, I didn't even know what a ghost *was* at the time!"

"Who was he?" she asked, smiling a little.

"My step-mother's dead brother," I answered flatly. "He was anchored to her, so he moved with her. He'd see other ghosts when she was outside and we worked out the rules together, when we were alone."

"Sounds… interesting…" she remarked.

"It wasn't," I refuted. "Because I didn't know that Benjamin was a ghost at the time, I talked and played with him like he was any other child. When my step-mother heard some of the things I knew about my 'imaginary friend' which included details I should *not* have known, she declared me evil and locked me up, beginning my time in hell…"

Emily sighed dramatically, dropping her head as she muttered, "Crappy childhood…"

"Yeah…" I muttered, more to myself.

"Okay, so…" she sighed, like she was still trying to come to grips with this. "After you see a ghost, do you, like, try to help them resolve their issues so they can move on, like they do on TV?"

"Um, no-o-o-o…" I drawled, drawing it out. "They do *what* on TV now?" I asked, not quite sure I heard her right.

"Well, in TV shows about someone that can see ghosts, they use their power to help ghosts so they can move on…" she answered, staring at me like I had just grown a second head.

"Yeah, I don't do that…" I sighed, feeling exhausted with this conversation.

"Why not?" she rebuked.

"Well, for one thing," I groused, "there are a *helluva* lot of ghosts out there, and for another thing, I can't be sure that where they're going will be *better* than their existence *here!* For all I know, what they face is oblivion! And, besides, if I spent *all* my time doing that, I'd end up in a psychiatric hospital and I'd rather avoid going back there…"

"Wait, *back?"* she gasped.

"Yes, okay, look…" I huffed. "I experienced something so horrible that my mind just kind of… shut down for a while, okay?"

I could feel myself edging closer to another damned flashback, so I reached over and grabbed Mr. Fluffybutt, my mismatched stuffed animal that was my secret weapon against my PTSD, and held him close, reveling in the feelings of love, safety, and peace I got from him.

Mr. Fluffybutt was created at a time before everyone agreed that bears would be the stuffed animal of choice. He was originally a rabbit, but his ears and signature fluffy tail had long since disappeared. His legs were unusually long for a bear, and one of his arms had clearly come from another stuffed animal. One of his eyes was the traditional large black button, but the other was a smaller, white, button that looked like it had come from a dress shirt. He had numerous stitches where parents had mended him and if he had ever had any fur, it was long since worn away. One of the few remaining things he had left from his early days was a leather collar with a brass plate with the name 'Fluffybutt' etched into it, giving testament to a name that would otherwise have been long forgotten.

As near as I could tell, Mr. Fluffybutt had been passed down older sibling to younger sibling, then from parent to child for at least five generations. I had snatched the little rabbit from the fate of being thrown away when a man had come into the antique shop hoping to sell the remains of an estate sale. The man was clearly an idiot that didn't know what a *treasure* Mr. Fluffybutt was!

"What's with the ugly bear?" Emily asked, looking repulsed at the treasure I held.

"Do *not* mock Mr. Fluffybutt!" I warned in my cold, serial-killer, tone.

Emily's eyes widened in horror and she backed away to the door.

"Mr. Fluffybutt is my most valued treasure," I whispered, looking away from Emily, while also trying to console her.

"Dammit Earl!" Emily muttered under her breath. "You *told* me not to endanger 'Mr. Fluffybutt' but you *neglected* to tell me it was damn stuffed animal!"

I confess I snorted at this, empathizing with her frustration with Earl.

"Okay, different topic," I sighed, feeling more at ease now that Mr. Fluffybutt was in my lap. "Every time I mention ghosts, you freak out. Why?"

"You wouldn't understand…" Emily sighed, putting a hand to her head.

"Probably not," I agreed ruefully. "But try me anyway."

"I grew up with two older brothers," she told me, as if this explained everything. When she saw my look of confusion, she continued, "They liked to scare me with ghost stories because when I would get scared, *they* would feel it, too, because…" she trailed off, waving her hand in front of her face.

"Why would they want to feel scared?" I asked, perplexed at the idea.

Emily gave me a look that screamed, 'are you *kidding* me?' then saw my face and sighed dramatically before answering. "Most people enjoy a good scare every now and then, as long as it's safe. Like watching a horror movie or riding a roller coaster."

"Neither of which I've done…" I confessed.

"You've never seen a *horror movie?"* Emily gasped.

"I've *heard* about them," I shrugged, "but I've never seen one. From what I've heard of them, they either seem really tame or don't portray ghosts the way they really are."

"Only you…" Emily muttered under her breath with a sigh.

"Probably…" I agreed, somewhat morosely.

I think it was around this time that I had trouble keeping my eyes open, so Emily let me be while I slowly fell into a doze. The rocking chair, plus Mr. Fluffybutt in my arms, not to mention the long and difficult day I'd had were all *more* than enough to send me over the edge into blissful sleep.

Chapter 4

Devil's Hour

I woke up stiff, cold, and hungry. The room was dark, the sun looking like it had set *long* ago. I felt around for my crutches and hobbled to a dizzy standing position.

My stomach and bladder were warring for attention. My bladder won, handily. I attended to my most urgent needs, then slowly made my way downstairs, inch-worming my way down the steps, convinced I would fall at any moment, break my neck, then end up haunting my own house.

It was with no small sigh of relief that I made it to the ground floor, whereupon Wendy greeted me, looking morose.

"What's wrong?" I asked the floating girl in a bare whisper, not wanting to wake up Emily.

"Emily made a mess in the kitchen..." Wendy warned me.

"We tried to stop her, but she couldn't hear us!" Peter complained loudly. To be fair, it's not like he had to worry about waking anybody up, except maybe Max...

"I'm sure it can't be *that* bad," I rationalized out loud.

Peter and Wendy just looked at each other, neither daring to say anything.

With a weary sigh, I made my way into the dining room, flicking on the lights to see Max's plate licked clean, along with a plate and glass that I assumed Emily had used, with a few remnants of what must have been her dinner.

Well, this wasn't so bad! She probably just didn't know where the dirty dishes went! I could deal with this after my midnight snack!

Wait... what time *was* it, anyway?

I made my way into the kitchen, flicking on more lights as I went. According to the oven, the time was sometime after three-am, sometimes known as the devil's hour...

Okay, blame my bible-thumping upbringing for me knowing this. Three-am is known as the devil's hour because it is believed, by *some*, mind you not by *me*, that Jesus was crucified at three-pm, so the opposite of that time, three-am, was believed to belong to the devil.

There. That's a thing you know now.

Okay, so it was either really late for a snack, or a little early for breakfast. Considering I had missed dinner, for which my doctors would be *horrified* to hear, I figured I was due for a decent-sized 'snack' even at this odd time.

The trouble is, Emily had also been in the kitchen to prepare her meal…

"Oh…" was all I could muster when I saw the work ahead of me. I saw a cutting board with bits of vegetable matter, carrots, cucumbers, and tomatoes from what I could see, a colander that looked like it had been used to rinse off lettuce, and a medium-sized pot that still held bits of dried beans, which had solidified into one hard mass at the bottom.

Well, I guess I should be grateful she hadn't used any of my cast-iron cookware… The mess with the beans, alone, could have ruined my Dutch-oven!

"You know what?" I sighed, dejectedly, "This mess can wait. Food first, cleaning later…"

I decided sandwiches would be a good snack, so I toasted up some bread in my toaster oven and dug out some thick slabs of leftover bacon, along with some mayo, mustard, and cheese. Once the bread had a nice, golden, toasting, I slathered it with mayo (the real kind, not the fake kind), along with some English mustard. I topped each piece with a slice of sharp cheddar before piling on some cold bacon. I ended up with two good-sized sandwiches. I set my plate with the sandwiches in the dining room, moving Emily's plate to make room for mine, before going back in the kitchen for a glass of milk. When I came back, I saw Max sitting in his regular seat, looking at me like I was some kind of traitor.

Alright, *fine!* I hobbled back into the kitchen, took what was left of my leftover bacon, and gave it a quick chop, putting it on a small plate and set it before Max. I got a satisfied purr for my efforts.

I sat down, panting a little by this time, and thoroughly enjoyed my bacon sandwiches. Judging by the way Max dug into his plate, I guessed he enjoyed his snack, too.

I took my time eating, both to savor the meal and to stall the necessary chore of cleaning I felt compelled to do afterwards.

When I felt I could no longer put it off, I took my plate and made my way into the kitchen. Since I needed one hand free, I ended up hobbling on one foot, leaning on my crutch with my other arm, and was deathly afraid I would drop something, or worse, fall flat on my ass.

Thankfully, the kids seemed to see my plight and a few seconds after I was back in the kitchen, the remaining plates and glasses in the dining room floated into the room, courtesy of Peter and Wendy.

"Thank you, kids," I whispered with smile.

Peter gave me a huge grin, while Wendy just blushed a little. I rinsed off the plates and placed them in the large dishwasher, leaving them there until there was enough for a full load. Next, I tackled the leftover foodstuff, sweeping the vegetable matter onto some paper towels before throwing them away.

Next came the challenge, the beans. I scraped out what I could, then used some dish soap on it before filling it with cold water to let it soak, leaving the soapy mound in one of the large sinks. The final task was wiping off the surfaces with a little disinfectant before calling it done.

Whew! That was… kind of exhausting… I made a note to talk to Emily about it the next chance I got.

So, what time was it now? I glanced at the clock on the stove and saw that it was just after four. Okay, so where did that leave me? I could either go back to bed, or I could stay up and do something at least semi-productive…

Well, I was out of breath, but I wasn't exactly tired… which made me lean towards semi-productivity, but the thought of any more physical work was out of the question…

I hobbled to the dining room, hoping for inspiration when I saw my laptop still sitting on the table. That settled things for me. I got the laptop booting up before grabbing my other crutch and going back into the kitchen to get some coffee going. Once there was enough coffee, I filled a thermos, which had the built-in cup, before heading back to the dining room and signing onto my language-learning subscription service.

Earl had been bugging me to start learning Korean, since we got some personal items from a recent Korean refugee that I helped rescue from the sex cult where I got shot. I had been using my recovery as an excuse to stall this demand, which was working so far, but this seemed like a good opportunity to get started on it, so I plugged in my headphones and microphone and got to work.

I have an exceptional memory, thanks to my horrible step-mother who whipped me for any hesitation in answering her questions. Earl has also told me that I have an ear for languages, proven to him when I repeated what I was hearing phonetically, without understanding what it meant. He actively encouraged me to learn as many languages as I could by promising me more pay with every language I mastered.

The money aside, I found learning new languages to be enjoyable. I imagine learning a new language, for me, felt the same as an athlete getting to run as they liked after being cooped up for so long. The strength and power of my mind seemed to make up for the weakness of my body.

Besides, when your whole life has been all about surviving to the next day, the joy that comes from doing something for the sheer *fun* of it is one of my treasured luxuries.

Yeah… the fact that learning a new language is fun for me sounded less weird in my head…

Before I knew it, I had gone through two thermoses full of coffee and I felt like I was finally getting my head around the grammar and alphabet of the language, which I always considered the two biggest obstacles in learning a new language. The rest is building vocabulary, which is largely just rote memorization, which I excelled at.

"You're up early!" Emily remarked, coming into the dining room. Max, who had been napping on a nearby chair, gave her a scowl and hissed when she tried to pet him.

"Got hungry, then felt like I had to get busy doing something," I shrugged.

"Oh? What are you doing?" she asked, sounding genuinely interested.

"Learning Korean," I answered, more-or-less, automatically.

"Korean?" she echoed, looking surprised.

"Yep," I replied, selecting the answer to a question on my screen. I checked the time and saw that I had been working on this for around five hours…

"Okay, I give up, *why* are you learning Korean?" she asked when she saw that I wasn't going to say any more.

"Remember the sex cult?" I asked, making her shake her head at what she thought was an abrupt change of topic. "Well, I was sent in there to rescue a girl that had been forced to marry a high official in North Korea. She got out with some of his personal things, which I can use to get into his head.”

“Okay, what does that have to do with learning Korean, though?” she asked, not quite following the logic.

I confess that I probably gave her an ‘are you serious?’ look, but answered her question anyway. “People tend to think in their native language. If I’m going to spy on a North-Korean, I need to know the language. Plus, it makes it easier to figure out what’s important and what’s not, to say *nothing* of reporting it all to the higher-ups.”

“Ah,” she mumbled, looking like she felt dumb for having asked.

“By the way…” I hesitated, knowing that what I was about to say might sound whiny, while also knowing it had to be said, “the next time you make something in the kitchen, would you mind cleaning up afterwards?”

“I always do!” she huffed, somewhat indignantly.

“You didn’t last time…” I rebuffed. “I’ve got the pan with the beans soaking now. I’m just glad you didn’t use my cast-iron cookware. Those require special treatment to clean.”

“Oh…” she blushed. “I guess I kind-of… forgot?”

“Just be mindful of it,” I shrugged, trying to make lighter of it than I felt. “And maybe don’t use the cast-iron…”

“You’ve really got a thing for food, don’t you?” she remarked, giving me an odd look.

I returned her look with a glare of my own suggesting she should already know the answer to that.

“Crappy childhood, right!” she sighed.

“How about I make us some breakfast?” I offered. “I’ve got some eggs, so I could…” I stopped, remembering that she might object to this, given that she was a vegetarian.

“Eggs are okay,” she smiled, looking like she had explained this before. “So are dairy foods and I don’t object to honey.”

“Okay,” I sighed with a little relief. “Then how about some egg, cheese, pepper, and onion frittata with some salsa on top? Oh, and maybe some buttered toast!”

“That seems like a lot of work for a breakfast…” she replied, giving me another odd look. She was just *full* of odd looks for me this morning!

“Less work than you think,” I shrugged. “The peppers and onion just need a quick chop, the cheese is already grated, and whisking the eggs is simple. Throw everything together into a skillet, then put the skillet in the oven, then slice and enjoy! Plus, it makes for some *great* leftovers!"

I confess I was probably salivating by this time, especially since I got a chuckle from Emily.

"Yep, obsessed with food…" she mumbled. "Is there anything I can help with?" she offered as I was getting up.

"Know how to make coffee?" I asked over my shoulder.

"Sure do!" she agreed, following me.

I got out the large cast-iron skillet and added some butter to the bottom before turning on the stove to get it heating up. Onions were first, since I wanted to caramelize them a little before adding everything else. Once the onions were chopped and cooking, I gave a red bell pepper a course chop before adding them to the pan and stirring it all together. I grabbed some eggs and gave them a quick whisking to scramble them before pouring them over the onions and pepper. The grated cheese was the last to go in, sprinkling a liberal amount over the top, then stirring them into the egg mixture. Last step was grabbing a towel to move the skillet into the heated oven to let it cook all the way through.

While that was cooking, I put the bread into my toaster oven (a gift from my foster-mother) that I adored, to get it toasting.

It was only then that I realized that Emily had been talking to me, though I hadn't heard a word of what she had been saying…

"Sorry," I cut her off. "When I'm cooking, I tend to…" I blushed at the confession, "block out everything else…"

"Yeah, I kinda figured that," she sighed, "especially after I said I was having your baby and you didn't bat an eye…"

I raised my eyebrows at this, then noticed that the bread was starting to brown a lovely golden color. I gave it maybe another twelve seconds, judging the hue until it was just right before opening the door and turning off the little toaster. I moved the bread onto a plate then added the butter I leave sitting out in a special butter container, so it's always soft. I gave each slice a good portion of butter and offered Emily two of the slices, which she took with a smile.

The frittata would be a while longer, so I took the time to enjoy my own toast, regretting a little that I didn't have an extra skillet, which would have allowed me to make Texas toast, which is to say bread fried in butter on a skillet. Oh well, the eggs would be more filling, anyway.

By the time I had finished the toast, and had a cup of coffee, the frittata was done. This time, I got Emily to pull it out of the oven with a towel I used *just* for handling the hot cast-iron cookware. We gave it a few minutes to cool off just a bit, while Emily set out the silverware and mugs of coffee in the dining room so that they'd be ready for us when we finally sat down to eat.

Emily finally cut the frittata into six pieces, took one, and was about to give me only one when I asked her to give me two.

"Two?" she asked, looking unsure I could eat that much.

"To start with," I shrugged, eyeing the meal hungrily.

"You know, if you eat that way, you're going to get fat!" she chided.

"Only if I'm lucky!" I shot back, smirking a little, since I knew she'd probably either hate me for it or wouldn't believe me.

"Well, you *are* kind of on the skinny side…" she agreed, not taking the bait.

"Docs say I need the calories," I agreed. "And the protein!"

"Of *course* they do…" she lamented.

After she had left for the dining room, I took one of the remaining pieces in the pan and cut it in half, setting it on a smaller plate before hobbling back to the dining room, setting the plate in front of Max, who was now looking expectant.

Emily eyed me, but didn't say anything, which was probably for the best.

We enjoyed a peaceful breakfast together.

If only it could have lasted…

Chapter 5

Part-Timer

Our peace was interrupted by my landline ringing.

"I'll get it!" Emily called, already dashing up to run to the living room.

"No, wait!" I shouted, already too late as I grabbed for my crutches.

"Hello? No, this is Emily, I'm a friend of hers…" I heard Emily speak into the phone. "No, she's busy at the moment, but maybe I can help?"

"Who is it?" I demanded in a harsh whisper.

Emily ignored me as she continued, "Oh! I could do that! I've worked retail before, so it'll be fine! Great! I'll be there in a bit!"

At this point Emily hung up the phone and I was furiously glaring at her.

"That was Anne, wasn't it?" I seethed.

"Yep! Seems she's in need of some part-time help!" Emily cheered.

"And you offered to help her out, didn't you?" I huffed, still pissed.

"Sure did!" she smiled, oblivious to why I was so angry.

To be fair, though, I was probably being a bit selfish in my anger towards her. Part of me didn't want her involved in my friends because I guarded them zealously, since I didn't have many of them and was always careful about making new ones.

"Fine, but I'm going with you!" I stated, leaving no room for argument.

"Oh, you don't have to!" Emily insisted. "I'll be perfectly fine!"

"I don't trust you not to manipulate my friends!" I sneered, viciously.

"Well at least you're honest about it…" she muttered, a tone of anger in her voice. "How about the customers? Can I at least practice what you told me on them?"

"Only if you're careful," I compromised. "Nothing too obvious, okay?"

"Scout's honor!" she promised.

"You were a scout?" I asked, packing up my laptop.

"It's just a saying..." she huffed, a little indignantly.

I slung my bag over my shoulder and we made our way out to her car. I, once again, gave her directions, though I'm pretty sure she knew the way. I mean, all the stores are lined up along one street, so all you need to do is head down that street and keep an eye open for pedestrians and the store you're looking for.

"It's more crowded than I thought it'd be," I remarked, a little idly.

"People have been getting stir-crazy after being locked up in their houses so long," Emily replied.

Oh yeah... the pandemic... kind-of forgot about that...

We ended up parking more than a block away and I was grumbling under my breath as we made our way up the street. Stupid cast, stupid crutches, stupid anemia...

I hate feeling so weak.

We finally made it up to the front of the store, though it probably took twice as long, since I was slowing Emily down. At least she didn't show the impatience I figured she would have.

Anne was busy at the register when we walked in, running a customer's card through the system.

"Anne, hi!" I called to the woman. Anne was in her late-forties, maybe early-fifties, and was kind of a spry matron. Her face was on the plain side, with only a little makeup, and her dress was decidedly conservative with a button-up shirt, with sleeves rolled up to her elbows, and slacks. Her hair was tied back in a business-like bun, with only a few strands escaping.

"Jane!" Anne cheered, looking relieved. "I'm sorry to call you like this, but I've been busier than I thought I would be and could really use the help!"

"Anne, this is Emily," I introduced, waving my hands a little in her direction. "She's the one you spoke to on the phone. I thought she could help out while I did some... *other* work, downstairs?"

Emily reached forward, shaking Anne's hand with a smile and Anne seemed to take it all in stride.

"I've got some new inventory downstairs that still needs to be priced," Anne told us, in-between customers. "After that, they'll need to be stocked on the shelves."

"How about I price them, then Emily can put them on the shelves?" I suggested. "Maybe after that, she could help out any customers in the store?"

"That would be great!" Anne agreed. "Just so you know, I paid ten dollars for the whole box down there, so keep that in mind when you're pricing them, okay?"

"I will," I promised, before motioning to Anne to follow me to the back of the store. I stopped at a locked door that led down to the basement. I dug out a key and unlocked it, gesturing for Emily to head down first, while I followed, locking the door behind me.

Emily was eyeing the large metal door set into a concrete wall.

"I didn't know storms were so bad here!" Emily gasped, looking at the bunker.

"It's not a storm bunker," I rebuked. "It's a SCIF room."

"What's a SCIF room?" she asked, oddly perplexed.

"It stands for Secure Compartmented Information Facility," I sighed, somewhat annoyed at having to explain something she should already know about. "It's where classified material can be safely sent, stored, and reviewed."

"And Anne just *let* the CIA build this down here?" Emily asked, clearly surprised.

"Anne doesn't own the store," I reminded her, pulling out wooden figurines from the box on the table.

"So, then, it's a CIA front!" Emily decided. "Huh! I wouldn't have figured they'd build one way out here! Is that why you moved out here?"

"I was here before the room was," I answered, somewhat absently as I looked over the wooden figurines. They looked to be hand-carved and hand-painted. Most were of anthropomorphized animals in cute outfits.

"Wait," Emily demanded, shaking her head like she had an unpleasant thought. "Are you saying they built *this* here for *you?*" she gestured at the bunker as if to show the large magnitude of the undertaking that must have happened.

"Pretty much," I remarked, trying to downplay the whole thing, as it was making me uncomfortable. "Earl complained that he wasn't able to do it at my house, since the kids tended to mess up electronics, so when the store came up for sale, I guess he bought it, figuring it would make a good front, not to mention make it more convenient for me to do my work, since I would always have a valid reason for being here."

Emily stared at me for a long moment, as if reassessing me before giving a dramatic sigh of defeat.

"What?" I demanded.

"I just…" she lamented, looking depressed. "I just didn't know what a big deal you are…"

I scoffed at this idea. "It wasn't like I had a choice…" I sighed, finding it hard to focus on the little wooden animals. "Earl found me after I found a missing girl. Made me an offer that was difficult to refuse. He promised me that I could save more kids that were lost, and alone, and desperately needing someone to come and save them. How could I turn *that* down?"

I wiped at my eyes, denying the tears that were threatening and studied the wooden animals, feeling them out with my other sense. I got the impression that they were all carved, and painted, by one person. I felt the subtle love a grandparent feels towards a grandchild. I counted at least two-dozen figurines that were small enough to fit in my palm, but large enough that I couldn't wrap my fingers around them.

"I think we could sell them for a dollar apiece," I judged, picking out a piece with an especially strong emotional link attached. This one was a penguin with a wreath around its neck, along with a red Santa hat on its head.

"We should advertise that they're hand-carved and painted," I added, setting the penguin aside to buy for myself later. I grabbed the price stickers and started writing the price on them before sticking them on the bottom of the figurines.

Emily joined in a moment later, making the work go quicker.

"So, you saving that penguin, there?" she asked, a little playfully.

"Gonna buy it and add it to the serenity room," I agreed.

"So *this* is where you get your stash!" she chuckled, good-naturedly.

"Guilty," I confessed with a small grin.

When we were done pricing them, I grabbed a blank sheet of paper, folded it in half, then wrote 'Hand-Crafted Figurines $1 each' on it to be placed on the shelf next to them.

"Now, then, where should I put these?" Emily asked.

"Wherever there's room," I told her. "But keep them together," I warned.

"I know, I know…" Emily sighed, somewhat dramatically before grabbing the box and heading towards the stairs. "By the way, what will *you* be doing?"

"Studying Korean," I answered nonchalantly.

"Ri-i-ight…" she drawled. "Should have known… overachiever…"

She was halfway up the stairs before I could dispute this, so I let it go.

The rest of the morning was quiet and I lost track of time, again, while working on my Korean lessons. At this point, I was getting most of the vocabulary down and making sure I was getting the grammar right. I figured if I worked at it, I'd be fluent enough to understand most of what was said before too long.

"Anne wants to know if you want me to pick you up something for lunch!" Emily called as she came down the stairs.

Lunch? What time *was* it? I checked my computer's clock and saw that it was noon! Hell and blast, I had lost track of time!

I took a deep breath and made sure I switched mental gears so I would speak in English, rather than Korean, before I answered her.

"There's a good burger place down the road that I think has salads," I mentioned.

"Sounds like it could work!" Emily agreed. "What can I get you?"

"A couple double-bacon-cheeseburgers, large fries, and a chocolate milkshake," I answered, digging out my wallet to make sure I had enough cash. I handed her enough paper money to cover it, which she took, giving me an appraising look.

"I hate that you can eat like that and still be so skinny…" she groused.

"It comes with a price," I lamented.

"Like what?" she scoffed.

"I bruise easily, heal slowly, and bleed profusely," I answered on automatic. "Plus my ability seems to burn through a lot of calories."

"Still seems like a good deal to me!" she rebuffed.

"And I get winded just walking down the street," I added with sigh. "If I stand up too quickly, I can black out, and I'm not allowed to drive. Also, I *literally* could not run to *save my life!"*

"Eh," she shrugged noncommittally before running back upstairs.

"Yeah, just go ahead and discount all the times I nearly died..." I huffed to myself, a little bitterly.

After I had my lunch, I was feeling drowsy, so I took a little nap on the small couch I had bought for the basement for this express purpose. Staring at the screen and learning so many new words was giving me a slight headache and wearing me out. Plus, now that I was comfortably full from lunch, my body decided it was a good time to demand time to put those resources to work. Who was I to disagree? Besides, the sooner my body healed my leg, the sooner I'd be out of the cast and the sooner my life could get back to something approaching normal.

"Sleeping on the job?" Emily snarked.

"Recovering from a serious injury," I disputed with a yawn before sitting up. "What time *is* it, anyway?"

"Coming up on four o'clock..." she answered, sitting on the cushion my legs had just vacated.

"Really?" I asked, a little dumfounded that I had slept so long. "Guess it's about time to go home, then..."

"Yeah, about that..." she hesitated.

"What did you do?" I demanded.

"I didn't *do* anything!" she replied, defensively.

I gave her a look that said I suspected otherwise.

"Okay, I *may* have invited the new deputy to our place for a card game..." she confessed.

"What new deputy?" I asked, completely unaware that Sheriff Carter had hired anyone.

"His name is John Hart and he is just *adorable!"* Emily squealed, sounding like she already had a crush on the man. "Think baby-face meets rugged cowboy!"

I confess I couldn't picture it... but whatever!

"Problem," I stated with a weary sigh. "The only cards I've got can't be used in a game."

"Why not?" she asked, a little confused.

"Because they're not normal cards," I told her, sighing as I figured I'd have to explain this a bit more. "They link to Earl's head and I doubt he'd appreciate me spying on him like that."

"So, we'll get some new cards! It's not like they're expensive!" she scoffed.

"I suppose…" I relented, not liking strangers in my house. "And I suppose I could make some snacks if it's just going to be the three of us…"

"Oh, it won't just be the three of us!" Emily remarked, her eyes going wide as she saw the dawning look of horror on my face.

"Who else is coming?" I asked in a forced cheery tone that would fool precisely *nobody*.

"Well, there's the sheriff," Emily counted on her fingers. "Then there's Anne, and her husband…"

I sighed with a little relief, but this was short-lived as she continued.

"But then that Beth lady showed up," she continued, eliciting a gasp of dread from me, which turned into outright horror at the last guest on the list. "And then she invited that Tim guy…"

"Aw hell and blast!" I snarled. "Beth and Tim are the *last* people I want in my house!"

"What's your problem?" Emily asked, sounding hurt.

"Tim is a conspiracy theorist," I answered quietly, working hard to keep my emotions in check. "And Beth already believes my house is haunted."

"But it *is!*" Emily countered.

"But I'd rather people didn't *believe* it was!" I hissed. "Do you know how *hard* it is to get delivery to my house? Everyone believes the house is haunted and that I'm some kind of *witch* for living in it!"

"So?" she scoffed. "Can't you get the kids to behave themselves? Don't you have some kind of power over them?"

"I have less power over them than *you* do over living people," I lamented. "I talk to them and I negotiate with them. *This* kind of negotiation, to get them to behave when there are so *many* people they could do mischief to will be… expensive…"

"What do you mean?" she asked, *finally* sounding worried.

"I mean," I sighed more dramatically than I had entirely meant, "games of hide-and-seek, tag, and catch, not to mention reading to them… Most of which would be exhausting when I *wasn't* in a cast!"

"Well, maybe I could cancel, or reschedule it for another time…" Emily offered.

"No…" I relented, thinking I might have been harder than I should have been. "Then I'd get a reputation for being unsociable… Just answer me this, *why* did you invite Tim Foyle *of all people* to the game?"

"I was kind of forced into inviting him," Emily confessed. "That Beth lady will *not* take no for an answer!"

Okay, yeah, that made sense. My anger at Emily deflated. After all, Beth had done the same thing to *me* several years ago, when she forced me to hold a séance at my house, right before a body had shown up at the cemetery… one that didn't belong there… at the time… long story…

"Yeah, Beth is like that…" I relented.

"Are you still mad at me?" Emily asked, looking anxious.

"Less mad, more… annoyed," I confessed. "I don't like strangers in my house, so I'd appreciate being consulted before you go inviting people over."

"Gotcha!" Emily nodded. "Next time, I promise I'll ask you first. Deal?"

"Deal," I agreed, sighing at the ordeal that was sure to come.

Six people, plus Emily and me, all playing cards at my house…

No good could come from this…

Chapter 6

Poker Face

Okay, so I had, basically *zero* time to prepare for an impromptu card game at my house which would include a total stranger, a gossip, and the man I least wanted to be locked in a room with.

Am I in hell? This *must* be what hell is like, right?

Emily drove us home and I raced into the house as fast as my crutches would let me, especially since I saw the sheriff's official vehicle right behind us the entire trip.

"Peter! Wendy!" I called somewhat louder than I had meant to. "We've got guests coming tonight, so I need you on your best behavior, okay?"

"Why should we?" Peter asked, petulantly. Of the two of them, Peter was more likely to get into shenanigans, which would likely bring suspicion to me.

"Because if you *don't,* then I *won't* read to you for a *week!"* I threatened, menacingly.

"Then we'll just have to *sing* when you're trying to *sleep!"* Peter countered, sticking his tongue out at me and making Wendy giggle.

I growled in frustration. Hell and blast, I did *not* have time for this!

"Okay, how about this?" I asked, getting desperate, "when my leg is better, I will play *tag* with the *two* of you for an *hour,* and *then* I'll play *hide-and-seek* for *another* hour, but *only* if you behave yourselves tonight! Deal?"

The two kids looked at each other with huge grins on their faces, nodded in unison, and shouted "Deal!" together!

The little brats… I was *seriously* hoping that they would forget this deal when the time came, but wasn't willing to bet money on it…

"So, will they behave?" Emily asked.

"Grudgingly," I answered, marching to the kitchen to find some kind of snack food for the guests. I had some homemade jerky that I like to keep handy, so I put some of that on a plate and handed it to Emily to put on the dining room table.

"The sheriff is at the door!" Wendy called from the entryway.

"And someone else!" Peter added.

"The sheriff and I'm guessing deputy are here," I echoed for Emily, gesturing for her to get the door.

Emily looked confused at first, probably trying to figure out how I knew, then made the connection as her face turned to one of shock and horror before finally forcing herself to calm down.

Part of me almost felt sorry for the woman, since she told me she *hates* ghost stories, and she now found herself *living* in one… Yeah, *almost*…

"Sheriff! Hi!" Emily called from the doorway as I stood, a little awkwardly in the dining room, unsure where I should sit.

Emily escorted the sheriff and new deputy into the dining room and I got my first look at John Hart.

Aw, hell and blast!

John Hart was tall and ruggedly handsome, with light brown hair that bordered on blonde, dark brown eyes, and a two-day stubble on a chiseled jaw. He looked to be in his early twenties yet he stood at least half-a-foot taller than I did, with muscles that were well-defined without restricting movement. His tan uniform looked tight on him, but in all the right places.

My heart felt fluttery and I wondered, idly, what kind of food he liked…

"John, meet Jane!" Emily introduced, somewhere far off.

John held out his hand and I shook it somewhat awkwardly. His grip was firm and when our minds connected, I got thoughts of finally seeing the inside of the famed haunted house of Amana, alongside thoughts of wondering how I had hurt my leg.

I worked hard to ensure that *none* of his thoughts showed on my face as I uttered a quick, "Nice to meet you!" to him.

John gave me a warm smile at this and I confess I probably blushed furiously. Oh, look! Dimples! Adorable little dimples!

Emily seated John quickly, placing her purse in the seat opposite him, marking her territory, the little demoness.

In short order, the rest of the guests filed in, with Anne and her husband arriving next, taking seats opposite each other at the far end of the table. Beth was next to arrive, holding bags of potato chips along with what I took to be gaming chips. Tim was last to arrive, dressed in a light red, almost pink, button-up shirt and dark jeans.

Sheriff Carter insisted on sitting to my immediate left, with Beth opposite her, while Emily insisted on sitting to my immediate right, with Anne just beyond her. Tim sat across from me, at the behest of Beth who looked like she was still trying to hook us up together for some reason that was beyond me.

I was worried about not having any cards to play with, but it turns out that about half the people that came had brought cards of their own, most in sealed packages.

"Um, I confess I don't, really, know how to play… poker was it?" I addressed the table at large once everyone had settled down and Beth started shuffling cards.

"You've never played poker before?" Tim asked, sounding surprised.

"It never came up," I blushed, feeling embarrassed. I confess that there are parts of my education that are woefully incomplete, while other parts, such as all things relating to the bible, are horribly *over*-complete.

Beth took this in stride and quickly explained the rules to me. Every player would get five cards, then bet using the poker chips which represented various money denominations, then they could exchange a number of cards to get new cards from the dealer. Those that had assembled the least-likely hand at the end would win.

Seemed simple enough, once I memorized the different types of hands you could have and their ranking. At first, I took it to be a game of chance, but as I played, I saw it was more about reading the other people at the table to judge the value of *their* hand in relation to the value of *your* hand. I could see that some tried to bluff, pretending they had a good hand, when they really had nothing.

After a few rounds, I thought I had the measure of the game well enough and I started taking it seriously. Soon enough I found myself winning almost every hand, which gained me some unwanted attention.

The sheriff took my hand, under the table, and whispered "Are you using your ability to cheat?" just loud enough that only she, and I through our link, could hear it.

'No,' I replied back to her without saying anything out loud. *'I'm reading faces, not minds.'*

The sheriff narrowed her eyes at me a moment before deciding I was telling the truth.

Immediately after the sheriff let go of my hand, Emily took my *other* hand and whispered, harshly, "Are the kids helping you *cheat?"*

I repressed my urge to growl at her and, instead, responded, *'The kids aren't helping me cheat! They're here, but they don't know how to play!'*

"Weren't they here when we explained to *you* how to play?" she asked, clearly disbelieving me.

'They were, but they weren't paying attention!' I replied, somewhat huffily. Seriously, is it *really* that difficult to believe that I could win so many hands *without* cheating?

'They're mostly just bored!' I added for good measure.

Emily eyed me closely, unsure if I was telling the truth, but finally relented.

Looking around, I could tell that they weren't the only ones that believed I might be cheating. I saw that Tim, who was suspicious by nature, was paying extra-close attention to me and my hands when he wasn't studying the walls and corners of the room, probably looking for hidden cameras.

It was then that I decided I had probably better start losing some rounds in an effort to allay some of the suspicion around me.

The conversation, up to this point, had been fairly light, with people talking about the weather, how it felt to finally be out of the house, and local sports. I hadn't really been paying attention to any of it, just making the appropriate sounds to show that I had heard and understood what was being said, but Tim changed all that.

"So, Anne, I've been looking into the company that bought your store!" Tim announced, which immediately made Anne, Sheriff Carter, and me tense up. Emily looked, more or less, at ease, probably figuring the CIA would have a good cover in place. I'm guessing Anne was less confident about this, while Sheriff Carter and I were nervous because we knew the *truth,* which is to say that I was the sole owner of the store.

"Oh?" Anne squeaked, looking flustered. I wanted to help the woman, but she was too far away from me to reach!

"I understood it was owned by some large corporation," I interjected, hoping this would be enough to help Anne out.

"That's the story," Tim agreed, "but when I looked into the company, it seems they only own one property, and that's the antique store."

"Really?" Beth, ever the one for gossip, inquired hungrily.

"Yep," Tim smirked, enjoying the spotlight. "The company was created just before the store went on the market, then bought it immediately afterwards."

"Interesting…" I added, finding it difficult to keep my voice from squeaking.

"Yeah, and from what I found out, I think it's someone local!" Tim announced.

"Why do you think that?" John Hart asked, sounding only vaguely interested.

"Because the address for the company is a PO box here, in town!" Tim declared, looking like he had just sprung a trap. "I've got someone staking out the box to see who shows up."

"Huh!" John Hart huffed. "I didn't think anyone in town *had* that kind of capital to throw around!"

"Well, I can only think of a few…" Beth threw in. "I mean, there's Jane, here, for one, and maybe one or two more, if they took out a loan…"

Tim's eyes locked onto mine, a look of surprise on his face. "I didn't know you had that kind of money!"

I swear by all that I have, I could have *murdered* Beth for that remark!

"I've got some money saved up," I confessed, trying to shrug it off like it was no big deal. "But I was in the hospital when the shop was bought. I was in that car accident, remember?"

"Oh, yes!" Beth chimed in. "She was gone for *months* that time!"

"Plus, I do other work… which helps out with my finances" I added, hoping to get him off my trail.

"Oh, what kind of other work?" Tim interrogated.

"I do some freelance translation work," I half-mumbled.

"Oh, I didn't know you knew other languages!" Beth smiled, chomping for more gossip.

"Just a few others," I chuckled, uncomfortably. "A friend got me a subscription to a language learning program online, so I thought I'd give it a try! Turns out, I've got a good ear for it."

"Really!" Tim smiled, possibly in an attempt to flirt with me. "What other languages do you know?"

"Well, aside from English, I know German and Russian," I answered, immediately seeing my mistake and trying to lessen it by adding, "and I'm dabbling in Japanese and Korean so that I can watch some cooking shows in their native language!"

"Huh!" Tim huffed. "German I can understand, given that this is a German town, but why Russian?"

"Well…" I struggled for a moment to come up with a plausible lie and came up with, "I heard it was challenging, what with its strange alphabet, and I like a challenge!"

Okay, yes, in hindsight, this was a damned *awful* lie, but it was the best I could come up on such short notice!

Tim looked unconvinced, at least for a while, but some faint tingling across my scalp told me Emily was working him hard. It took all too long for Tim's face to go from skeptical to grudging acceptance.

The rest of the card game was especially tense, at least for me. Part of that was because Tim looked like he wasn't entirely convinced and part of that was from Emily using her ability on John Hart to flirt with him!

I'd call her out for cheating, but she *had* just, sort-of, saved me back there, at least a little… Plus, she had seen him first, so she sort-of had dibs on him?

I ended up losing the rest of the hands, more or less on purpose. Honestly? I just wanted it all to be over. This card game had been an all-around disaster and the sooner it ended, the better.

So, for those keeping score at home, by the end of the game, Tim had become ever *more* suspicious of me, while the new heartthrob, John Hart, was being pursued by my housemate, who I was coming to blame for this whole fiasco, and I was still stuck in a cast, feeling weak and tired…

Honestly, what had I done to deserve all this?

Chapter 7

Trouble Brewing

With the game over, and the small-talk dwindling, people started leaving, much to my relief. Anne and her husband were the first to leave, followed by Tim, then Beth. John looked reluctant, but the sheriff encouraged him by saying they'd have an early day of it tomorrow.

I could tell that the sheriff wanted to talk to me by the way she kept eyeing Emily, looking like she was wondering just who she was to me.

"I figured the two of you already met, but in case you haven't," I mentioned by way of introduction, "Sheriff Carter, meet Emily Pathos, with Project Aesop."

"I was wondering if she was one of yours…" the sheriff commented wryly.

"Jane!" Emily hissed, looking pissed. "You can't just go around *telling* people about that!"

"The sheriff already knows," I explained wearily. "She knows most of my secrets, come to think of it…"

"Earl pays me to keep an eye on her," Carter added unhelpfully.

"Look, just because I ran off that *one* time!" I whined.

"As I recall, you got *stabbed* that one time!" the sheriff countered.

"You got stabbed?" Emily asked, looking shocked.

"It was just in the arm!" I rebuked. "It wasn't that bad!"

"Maybe, but perp-walking the man into the precinct with an arm covered in blood?" the sheriff quirked an eyebrow at me, "that seems excessive!"

"The blood stop powder was doing its job and keeping the bleeding down to a minimum," I moaned. "And I really didn't want him to get away while I went to the hospital to get stitches!"

"But… don't the cops know who you are now?" Emily asked, looking concerned.

"I wasn't Jane at the time," I sighed. "I was Agent Dreamer with the FBI."

"Wait!" Emily demanded harshly. "You've got an alias with the *FBI?*"

"Well… *yeah!*" I scoffed. "As Dreamer I've got more access to case files, which I need to catch psychic criminals!"

"Which you *don't* need, since you can look through Earl's eyes, remember?" Emily countered.

"But looking through his eyes means I also hear his *thoughts,* which I'm not cleared for!" I shouted, getting angry that she was arguing with me. "And asking him to school his thoughts for so long is asking too much of him, okay!"

I was starting to pant with all the shouting, driving my dislike for the woman even further.

"Besides, I can read people better than he can," I mumbled to nobody in particular.

"All of which is *beside* the point!" the sheriff stated, looking like an exhausted parent breaking up an argument between two kids.

"What *is* your point?" Emily demanded, not giving up the fight.

"I blew it with Tim, didn't I?" I lamented.

"You sure as hell did!" the sheriff huffed. "Honestly, what were you *thinking* telling Tim that you spoke *Russian* and were learning *Korean*?"

"I also told him I knew German and was learning Japanese!" I wailed, somewhat pitifully.

"Neither of which he's going to *care* about!" the sheriff shouted.

"Come on!" Emily pleaded. "What's the worst that can happen?"

"Well, Tim could post a crazy story about me to his blog," I ticked off on my fingers.

"And it doesn't even have to be *true* to cause trouble," the sheriff added.

I nodded at the sheriff in agreement. "Which means that Beth will read about it," I continued, moving onto my second finger.

"Which means that before long *everybody* will know about it," the sheriff nodded, moving onto the next point, which I dutifully marked by pointing to my third finger.

"And if the *wrong* people find out about me," I moved onto my fourth finger, "then I'll have to bug out and start my life all over again somewhere else!" I finished, pointing to my thumb.

"NOOOOOO!!!!" the kids wailed in fury!

The temp in the room dropped to near freezing as chairs started moving on their own, the table started shaking, and the chips in the bowl started flying around the dining room!

I covered my ears totally ineffectually, since ghost voices bypass my ears and run straight into my head.

"But that won't happen because we'll call Earl and warn him about it so he can stop that from happening!" I shouted as loud as I could, trying to get the kids' attention.

"You don't have to *shout!*" Emily complained loudly as the noise from the kids died down to sniffles and the odd wail.

"I kinda did," I sighed, grateful that I could hear myself again.

"The kids didn't like that, did they?" the sheriff asked, looking sympathetic.

"Nope!" I agreed. "Not one bit!"

"Come on, though!" Emily scoffed. "How close to the truth could he *get?"*

"He doesn't *have* to get to the truth!" I growled.

"Remember Mr. Boday?" the sheriff asked, smirking a little.

"Who's Mr. Boday?" Emily asked, looking a little nervous.

"I ran into him while walking down the street," I started, disliking this particular tale. "He was being haunted by the ghost of his wife, who kept screaming that he had killed her. I… might have freaked out, a little."

"And?" Emily prompted.

"And then he was found murdered in the cemetery with numbers burned into his arm," I finished.

"It didn't help that people found out while you were holding a séance here," the sheriff smirked, enjoying this a little too much for my liking.

"Beth was the one holding the séance," I corrected. "Anyway, Mr. Boday's friend started accusing me of murdering him, not to mention telling people that I was some kind of witch, or something. He even got his *kids* involved!"

"The whole *town* was talking about it!" the sheriff threw in, unhelpfully.

"So I had to get involved," I sighed. "I had to clear my name and hunt down the *real* killer. That's when Agent Dreamer was born."

"And then she captured the Cryptic Killer," the sheriff finished.

"Wait, that was *you?*" Emily asked, sounding gobsmacked.

"He was the first serial-killer I caught, yeah…" I shuddered, remembering that damned graveyard on Halloween night of all nights!

"So… how many serial-killers have you caught, then?" she asked, giving me a strange look, like she was trying to reconcile what she was hearing with how I acted.

"Um…" I hesitated, counting them up. "Let's see… there was the Cryptic killer… the Chicago Cannibal society…" I repressed an involuntary shudder at this mention, but I took a deep breath and continued, "the Black Scorpion, the Locked Room Killer… those three for sure, but I don't think they ever considered Randall Bishop a serial-killer even though he worked a *lot* of people to death, so I still think he should count!"

I confess I hesitated mentioning the Chicago Cannibal society

Emily was wide-eyed at my pronouncement, looking seriously concerned.

"You know," she mused, "for someone that shouldn't be out in the field *at all,* you sure do get around!"

"Well, I got involved with the Cryptic killer because of a prophet," I sighed, remembering the drunkard Jeremiah. "He told Project Aesop that if I *didn't* get involved, more people would die. Even so, I couldn't save his last victim…"

"Now, I've heard of the Chicago Cannibal society…" Emily started, wincing at my involuntary shudder at the mention of it, "but I've never heard of the Black Scorpion…"

"He was a Russian agent," I explained. "A psychic with the ability to bring pain with a touch. He was hunting down members of Project Aesop, sending them into pain-induced comas. "He was coming after a friend of mine, who *had* been staying here at the time, but was gone by the time the Black Scorpion got here. Earl and the kids ambushed him just outside. He got away, but he left some blood behind. That was enough for me to get into his head and bring him down."

"How?" Emily asked, looking confused.

"With Betty Tightwad," I answered, tears threatening my eyes.

"Who?"

"The Chicago Cannibal Society's last victim," the sheriff answered for me. I think it was obvious that I was on the brink of a flashback, so she was doing what she could to help out.

"Anyway," the sheriff continued loudly, clearly directing a change in topic. "Did you hear that Tim is staking out the post office?"

"Yeah, I heard…" I moaned. "Dammit, Tim!"

"So?" Emily scoffed. "What's so bad about that? You don't think the CIA will get caught like *that* do you?"

The sheriff gave me a look that clearly said she was going to leave *me* to answer this question.

"The CIA doesn't own the shop," I sighed. "*I* do."

"Wait," Emily shook her head, trying to come to grips with this. "I thought you said you were in the hospital at the time! A car accident, wasn't it?"

"I was in a psychiatric hospital at the time," I corrected a little mournfully. "It was right after the Chicago incident. I had set up an LLC with a lawyer, making him my proxy, right after I heard Anne talking about maybe selling the store. I had my lawyer buy it as soon as it came on the market."

"*You* bought the store?" Emily gasped.

"Don't tell Anne!" I commanded.

"But…" Emily spluttered. "How did you get the money?"

"I can't tell you," I stated, flatly.

"*Can't* or *won't?*" Emily demanded.

"Look, I signed an NDA, okay?" I hissed. "If I tell you, I'll lose it all!"

"Just what kind of shady deal did you make?" Emily accused.

"Nothing shady!" I shouted. "It was all completely legal!"

"Su-u-ure it was!" she drawled, rolling her eyes.

"It probably was legal, if my suspicion is right!" the sheriff smirked.

"So? What was it?" Emily demanded of the sheriff, now.

"It was a grant from a legitimate foundation," the sheriff answered, vaguely.

"And that's all you're going to tell her, *right?* " I hissed at the sheriff.

Look, I know I might have been protecting the secret a little more than was absolutely necessary, but the foundation had literally saved me in more ways than one, so I felt I owed it to them to protect them as much as I could.

Besides, anyone that knew me as well as Emily *ought* to have, by this point, should have been able to figure it out! After all, I'm certain the sheriff had!

"So, what are we going to do?" the sheriff asked, trying to get us all back on topic. "You know it's only a matter of time before Tim does something stupid and exposes you, right?"

"I'll call up Earl," I announced. "He's probably already keeping an eye on Tim, but it's better if he knows to watch out for anything he's *about* to publish."

I got out my cell phone and dialed this week's contact number.

"Shake City, where we shake up your sweet tooth!" came the cheery answer.

"Sorry, wrong number!" I answered, mocking their cheer. "I was trying to reach *Snake* City!" I promptly hung up, then set the phone on the table, waiting for Earl to call me back.

"Does Earl do this to you, too?" the sheriff asked Emily, idly, while we waited for the phone to ring.

"Pretty sure he does this to everybody," Emily sighed. "Truthfully? I pity the people on the other end! Imagine getting somebody that *wasn't* a spy!"

Before she could continue this thought, though, my phone rang, with the caller ID showing a blocked number.

"Hello?" I answered into the phone, certain it was Earl, but not wanting to get chewed out by Earl *again* for not feigning ignorance.

"It's Earl," he announced alertly. "Report!"

"Tim was at my house," I explained, doing my best to stay calm. "During the conversation I... *may* have told him that I'm fluent in Russian and was learning Korean... Pretty sure Tim is suspicious of me now. He's also hunting down the owners of Anne's Antiques and said he's staking out the post office to see who opens the post office box."

"I *told* you you were being too careless with that!" Earl chided.

"Well he hasn't caught me *yet!*" I huffed. "But I thought you should know that I get the impression he's gearing up to slander my name..."

"I've been keeping an eye on him," Earl went for reassuring, but missed the mark just a bit. "I have measures in place in case he tries to post anything about you, but I'll be extra vigilant, now."

"I don't want to know," I stated in a monotone, more certain of this than anything else in this call.

"It's better that you don't!" Earl sneered. I could practically *hear* that damned smirk on his face!

"Just don't get caught doing anything illegal," I countered. "And leave my name out of it!"

"Count on it," he stated before disconnecting.

Promises, promises...

Chapter 8

The Tinfoil Hatter

I spent the next six days trying not to worry about what Tim Foyle might be up to. I focused on learning Korean, eating, and sleeping. I may not be able to keep my body busy, but I sure kept my mind occupied.

I also took a few preventative measures, such as getting Earl to pick up any letters at the post office box and bringing them to the store. I let Emily do part-time work for me while I stayed home, only filling in when work got hectic, which wasn't often.

Then the shit hit the fan.

Tim posted an article titled 'The Russian Sleeper and the Agent in Black Tracking Her.'

As far as titles go, it's anything but poetic, but damn did it get the point across!

I got an alert on my phone that Earl helped me set up about the article. I spent the next ten minutes reading it before dialing up Earl, using the cutout he had in place, but by the time I got Earl on the line, the article had already been taken down.

It had been up for all of about twenty minutes, but it felt like twenty *years!* I felt the world drop out from under me while reading that *damned* 'article' that Tim had written!

The gist of the article was that there was a mysterious Russian sleeper agent living in a small town in the Midwest. Wherever this mysterious person goes, something big pops up in the news, along with reports of an older Agent in Black that seems to be tracking this spy. Tim theorized that this Agent in Black was tracking the Russian spy, but has been unable to track them to their home base, where Tim is writing from.

The evidence that he cites was all circumstantial, but damning, nonetheless. He wrote that this agent had an obviously fake name, and was able to buy a large house without need for a loan, through some unknown source of income. Add to that this agent's unknown, or altogether vague past, not to mention that they were fluent in languages a Russian sleeper agent would be expected to know, and he was starting to convince *me* that I might be a sleeper agent, after all!

He went on to cite that this agent is sometimes gone for *months* at a time, supposedly while they were in a hospital, but he threw out there that they might be going back to Russia to make their reports. What's more, this agent had a strange new house-mate that might be their new handler, or maybe a replacement!

There was also talk about how this agent had infiltrated the local law-enforcement, possibly blackmailing the sheriff to work for them, since the sheriff had once arrested them, then immediately let them go! The sheriff had even *apologized* for arresting them, when they had every reason to think them suspicious!

The final paragraph of the article had Tim calling for the Agent in Black to contact him so that he can point them in the right direction and arrest this Russian spy.

All-in-all, it was pretty damning, when you didn't have the whole story... The trouble is, Tim had never even *bothered* to ask me for *my* side or let me explain!

Not that I *could* have explained much... There are large chunks of the story that I would either have to stonewall the man on, or outright lie to his face should he ask me about them...

Aw hell and blast! Dammit, Earl! Call me back!

As if Earl was psychic, a blocked number showed up on my phone.

"Hello?" I huffed, trying, and failing, to keep the anger and stress out of my voice.

"I know, I know!" Earl pleaded, sounding like he was having the same problem I was having with keeping his voice neutral. "The bastard is trickier than I thought he was!"

"What happened, Earl?" I demanded.

"I thought we had all the servers he was using, but he surprised us with a new one!" Earl explained, his voice strained.

"But the article is gone, now, right?" I begged. "It won't be coming back?"

"It's off the main site, but who knows how many people saw it?" Earl groused.

"What happens if the wrong people saw it?" I asked, knowing I'd hate the answer.

"We can set you up somewhere else," Earl promised, or maybe warned.

"Dammit Earl!" I shouted, tears threatening to break free. "I can't just *leave!*"

"And I can't have you as a sitting duck!" Earl growled. "You're too valuable an asset to the organization! Even if the Russians don't know who you really are, all this talk of a Russian sleeper agent is *bound* to get them snooping around, and when they *do* and they discover that you're enemy number one with Prizrak, do you *know* what they'll do to you?"

"They'll kill me…" I whined.

"Only if you're *lucky!*" Earl shot back, making me gasp. "They're more likely to take you *prisoner* then try to use you to bring down Project Aesop, or maybe try to turn you to their side! Dammit, Jane! You *know* they're not above using torture! Remember the Black Scorpion?"

"How could I forget?" I mumbled, quietly, wanting to *strangle* Tim for what he had done to me!

"Well, their other interrogators aren't so *nice* as him!" Earl retorted. "The Black Scorpion only made you *think* you were feeling pain, without damaging your body! The others, though, would use specially-designed instruments to inflict minimum damage to your body while making you scream in agony."

"So, what are you going to do about Tim?" I asked, feeling reluctant to know the details.

"I *want* to arrest the bastard for *treason!*" Earl answered, his voice turning cold. "But I may have to settle for scaring the living shit out of him!"

"What should I be doing, then?" I asked, feeling helpless.

"Keep that app I gave you up and running and keep an eye on Tim," Earl answered with a sympathetic sigh. "I'll keep tabs on him, too, but it doesn't hurt to have another set of eyes on him. "Beyond that, plead ignorance about the article. Don't let him know that you read it, or else he might think you've been watching him because you see him as a threat."

"But I *do* see him as a threat!" I shot back, panic choking my voice.

"But he doesn't *know* you're onto him!" Earl explained, somewhat wearily. "If you're going to play the innocent victim, like you *should,* then you can't go acting like a predator with him."

"Do you know how many people saw the article?" I asked, meekly.

"I don't…" Earl confessed.

"Aw hell and blast!" I muttered before disconnecting.

I hated feeling so damned helpless, but what could I *do* about it?

Well, I could go over and *strangle* Tim, but then I'd get arrested, and it would be just my luck that Tim's ghost would haunt me. Not to mention all the ghosts that are bound to be anchored to any prison they send me to… to say *nothing* of the horrible food they're reputed to have there…

Oh, and I didn't do it because murder is *wrong*; that, too!

Chapter 9

Sarah Foxx

Shortly after I got off the line with Earl, I got a call I wasn't, entirely, expecting, though in retrospect, perhaps I *should* have…

"Afternoon, Sarah," I greet into my phone.

"Jane, I'm coming over!" Sarah declared, decisively.

"Sarah, wait!" I pleaded.

"No argument!" she asserted, disconnecting.

"Aw, hell and blast!" I moaned to myself.

"What's wrong?" Wendy asked, looking concerned.

"Nothing, exactly," I told her, trying to mollify them, which only made Wendy look *more* concerned. "Okay," I acceded, "Tim wrote an article about me that accused me of being a bad person, and now I think some bad people will see it and come after me. Earl is going to try to get Tim to see the error of his ways, while Sarah is coming out, probably to try to help me, somehow."

"We can help!" Peter declared confidently.

"That's sweet," I tell him, tenderly, "but the two of you are sort-of stuck here and I'm the only one that can see you…"

"Well, if he comes here, he'll regret it!" Peter smirked, a malicious look on his face.

"No maiming!" I commanded. "Or killing!" I added for good measure. "If you see him, bumps and bruises *only!* Am I clear?"

"O-okay…" the two drawled, looking somewhat disappointed.

"I'll tell you what," I sighed, feeling a need to comfort them, "I'll read to the two of you tonight, after Sarah gets here, but *only* if you behave yourselves, okay?"

"Yay!" the two of them cheered before flying off to who knows where.

Well, if Sarah was coming over, she'd probably want to stay the night, given that it's a three-hour drive between Omaha and Amana, and it was already coming up on noon. I guess I'd better prepare a room for her…

I inched my way up the stairs, found the room Emily was using and picked another room that was, more or less, clean. I tossed a crutch on the bed and awkwardly grabbed a broom to sweep up the hardwood floor with one hand, while using my other hand to stay upright.

I was panting before I was halfway done.

"Emily's back!" Wendy called, floating up through the floor.

"Oh good!" I cheered, grateful at the possibility of some more help. "Thank you, Wendy!"

Wendy giggled at this and I moved to the hallway, listening for Emily to come in the front door. When I heard the door shut, I called down, "Hey, Emily! Welcome back!"

"Jane?" she questioned, sounding confused. "Where are you?"

"Second floor!" I called back. "Come on up! I could use your help with something!"

I watched with a little envy as she made her way quickly up the stairs.

I hate feeling weak…

"Jane? What's going on?" she asked, looking concerned.

"I got a call from Sarah," I told her. "She's coming over and will probably be staying the night."

"Okay, who is Sarah and why is she coming over, much less staying the night?" she asked, sounding befuddled at the abrupt turn of events.

"Tim posted an article about me," I started, with a small sigh. "He didn't name me *specifically,* but he put enough out there that anyone that personally knew him, or me, would know it was about me. Earl got the article down, but Sarah, my foster mother, saw it and now she's coming over."

"Oh!" Emily mumbled, her mouth gaping in shock. "How long until she gets here?"

"A bit over two hours from now," I answered, collapsing into a sitting position at the foot of the bed. "It's a long drive from Omaha," I added, figuring it would be the next question she'd ask.

"How much does she know?" she asked, sounding guarded.

"She knows about ghosts and the fact that I'm a psychic," I answered, matter-of-factly. "She also knows I work for the CIA and *probably* knows most, if not all, of the cases I've worked on, or been involved in."

"Does she know about Dreamer?" she asked, quirking an eyebrow.

"I don't think I've told her about that," I decided after a moment's thought. "But it wouldn't surprise me if she figured it out on her own. That's how she knows about most of the bigger cases, at any rate."

"Okay, so what about me?" she asked, sounding nervous as she bit her lower lip.

"She's probably cleared to know about you," I told her, trying to wave off her concern. "She works as an editor for the Cy Magus Foundation," I threw in, though I'm not sure why. Maybe I wanted her to take the hint about where I got all my money.

"Sounds like she's the *last* person you'd want to be around!" Emily scoffed.

"Why?" I wondered.

"Because she sounds just like Tim!" she chuckled.

"In what way?" I asked, genuinely befuddled.

"All these weird theories about what's *really* going on with all these psychics, when the truth is staring her in the face!" Emily was practically guffawing by now!

I let out a long sigh before telling her, in no uncertain terms, "Most, if not *all,* of the psychics you see on TV *are* frauds. Sarah helped me find my place after I ran away from home. She got me into the system, got my name changed, and dealt with my cruel father and evil step-mother. She gave me the education I needed, going so far as hiring private tutors to get me my GED. I only stayed with her a few years, but I wouldn't *be* here if it wasn't for her kindness. She *literally* saved my life! So, *please,* be nice to her, okay?"

I grabbed my other crutch and made a hasty exit from the room before she could answer. I inched my way back down the stairs and retreated to the dining room, feeling like a coward as I wiped tears from my eyes.

I'm not sure how long I sat there, coming to grips with the intensity of my emotions. I could probably have used Mr. Fluffybutt just then, but he was still up in the serenity room, which might as well be on the other side of town, in my condition.

Heh! Dr. Theodore Bear, or doctor Teddy bear as I liked to think of him, would call Mr. Fluffybutt another kind of crutch… He'd gently chastise me for relying on the rabbit so much, while encouraging me to handle the emotions I was feeling on my own, to recognize and acknowledge them.

Okay, so what *were* my emotions, then? Well, I was feeling anger at Emily for what I saw as belittling a woman I had a great deal of respect for, but was she *really?* Maybe Emily just figured that Sarah was just another part of my crappy childhood and I ran away from her as soon as I could because I wanted to get away from her! From what I could tell, Emily has pretty much always known about her ability and her brothers, at least, acknowledged, and even *accepted* it, even if they *did* try to take advantage of it by scaring her with ghost stories for a harmless scare.

Aw, hell and blast! I was blowing her statements all out of proportion! I just *assumed* that she had seen the warning signs I felt sure I was giving off, because I forgot that she can't read people as well as I can!

"I'm beginning to see why Earl made *you* senior agent, here!" Emily announced from the doorway, looking uncomfortable, like she was walking on eggshells around me.

"Oh? Why's that?" I asked, keeping my voice a monotone.

"He told me that some of the agency's best agents come from broken homes," she answered, staring at me intently, perhaps trying to read my mood. "These agents are broken as children, then they reform themselves into something new, and are harder at the places where they're broken."

I shrugged noncommittally.

"Sarah's the closest you've ever come to having a childhood, isn't she?" she asked, seemingly out of the blue.

"More or less," I agreed. "I got a glimpse of what it must be like to have someone who cared about me. I guess that's why I'm so protective of her…"

"I'm sorry," she lamented. "When you told me about her, I just…" she tapered off, perhaps ashamed of her own thoughts.

"You thought she was another part of my crappy childhood," I finished for her. "And you couldn't see how tense I became when you compared her to Tim…"

"Yeah…" she sighed, looking miserable.

"Sorry," I huffed, forcing myself to become cheerful. "I guess I forget that others can't read people as well as I can!"

"Heh! *That's* for sure!" she smirked. "How *do* you do that, anyway?"

"Evil step-mother," I shrugged. "If I didn't read her well, she'd whip me with a bamboo switch. Survival is pass-fail. You pass, you live; you fail, you die. I passed."

"Well, at least you got some useful skills out of it," Emily sighed.

"I guess…" I shrugged, not really agreeing with her assessment.

"So, forgive me?" she asked, looking hopeful.

"Only if you forgive me for blowing up at you," I agreed.

"Deal!" she declared, holding out her hand. I looked at her hand a little suspiciously. Did she forget that me touching her hand meant I'd be in her head or was she trusting me that much?

Aw, what the hell! I shook her hand, feeling her satisfaction at this talk.

"By the way," she added with a smile. "The room is ready for her."

"Thank you for that," I smiled back. I checked the time. It looked like it would be another hour before she'd be here. Hell and blast! Had I *really* spent so long psychoanalyzing myself?

We spent the next hour, or so, talking about the article, since Emily hadn't seen it. She laughed when Tim posited that she was my new handler and *might* have muttered something like, "more like the other way around…"

I also checked in on Tim's location, using the app Earl had given me. It looked like Tim was home at the moment. I reminded myself to check the app much more often to avoid bumping into him accidentally. I didn't trust myself not to beat him senseless with one of my crutches and I couldn't afford breaking one of them! I mean, do you know how *hard* it is to get around with only *one* crutch?

Oh, and beating up people is wrong…

"Sarah's here! Sarah's here!" Wendy called, flying into the room.

"Sounds like Sarah's here," I told Emily.

"I didn't hear anyone drive up," Emily retorted.

"Neither did I!" I sang, darting my eyes upward so she'd figure out how I knew.

"Ghosts! Right… shoulda figured…" she muttered, getting up to get the door.

I followed her, looking out one of the windows to see Sarah's sizeable sedan. Sarah is an older woman, perhaps fifty or so, with dark brown hair and eyes. She's a bit taller than I am, but is on the healthier side of plump, while I'm more on the dangerously skinny side of healthy. I saw her reach the bottom step of the porch before stopping dead in her tracks as she saw Emily.

I'm not sure what Sarah made of Emily, but judging by the look on her face she was debating whether she should run or fight.

It was time to intervene, so I came up behind Emily and waved to Sarah, shouting, "Come on in and I'll introduce you!"

Sarah relaxed, a little, at this and came up the steps, much to the rejoicing of Peter and Wendy, though nobody but me could hear them.

I herded them to the dining room for introductions.

"Sarah, meet Emily Pathos," I introduced, nodding at Emily. "She's a psychic that's staying here in-between jobs. Emily, this is Sarah Foxx, my foster mother."

"Nice to meet you!" Emily greeted, holding out her hand. Immediately, my scalp erupted with an army of ants running in a mad-dash.

"Stop that!" I hissed at Emily, furiously scratching my head with both hands.

"Sorry!" Emily pleaded, looking chagrined. "Reflex!" she added.

"What's going on?" Sarah asked, jerking her hand back.

"Emily is a strong broadcaster that can influence people's emotions," I explained.

"Well, everyone except Jane!" she huffed.

"Yeah, it feels like bugs crawling over my scalp!" I threw in, wiping my hair back in place.

"Interesting…" Sarah murmured. "I wonder why that is…"

"There's a few theories out there," I answered. "One is that I'm such a strong broadcaster, in my own right, that it overpowers the abilities of others. The other theory is that the

Chicago incident forced me to build strong mental defenses just to get by.”

“The one that sent you to the hospital?” Emily asked, looking like she only vaguely remembered.

“For nearly six months,” I agreed, making Emily’s eyebrows shoot up in surprise. “I told you it was bad. My mind shut down almost completely. I might still be there if it wasn’t for Mr. Fluffybutt and Dr. Bear!”

“And they wouldn’t even let me in to see her!” Sarah protested.

“I wasn’t safe,” I chided quietly. “Trust me, you do *not* want those memories accidentally getting into your head!”

“Besides,” Emily threw in with a shrug, “they were probably worried she might say something she wasn’t supposed to, to someone who wasn’t cleared for it!”

“Yeah, that’s what Earl kept saying…” Sarah groused.

“Look, if it helps,” I sighed, “I wasn’t lucid most of the time. I probably wouldn’t have recognized you. I *barely* remember my time there, and then only the last month or so when they had me in physical therapy.”

Sarah sighed, looking only partially mollified.

“So, how much of the article did you read before Earl brought it down?” I asked, hoping a change in subject would change her mood.

“I saved it,” Sarah answered. “I’ve read it several times now. He doesn’t name you, specifically, so it might not be libel, but you might want to get a lawyer to check it out.”

“It would have to be a lawyer with clearance,” Emily suggested.

“That’s part of the rub,” Sarah agreed. “Another part is proving damages to you or your reputation.”

“Earl told me to pretend I hadn’t seen the article,” I declared. “After all, the Jane Doe that’s totally innocent wouldn’t have an alert for that kind of article, much less think it related to her.”

“Fair point,” Sarah conceded. “So, what are you going to do now?”

“Short term? I’ve got a Korean proficiency test tomorrow,” I answered. “After that, I’ll probably be poking around a Korean official’s head tomorrow afternoon.”

"What *is* the time difference between here and Korea?" Sarah asked, ever the pragmatist.

"Korea is fourteen hours ahead of us," I answered, having looked up the time difference just after I started learning the language. "So, I'd probably have to work at around six pm, then try to get a quick nap in before a shift at the store, come back around mid-day for dinner, then conk out until six again."

"Sounds rough!" Emily gasped.

"Comes with the territory," I shrugged. "It'll also depend on the official's schedule. If he spends a lot of time at parades or goofing off, then I can skip those in favor of a nap."

"Isn't there some way around it?" Sarah asked, looking concerned, perhaps eyeing the bags under my eyes.

"Not really," I lamented. "My ability works in real-time, so the only way around it would be to move to South Korea, or something, and that's out of the question."

Sarah gave me an odd look that suggested she might be thinking that I stretch myself too thin keeping two jobs. She might be right, but Earl wasn't about to let me quit the work I was doing with him, and I couldn't give up my job at the antique store, not when I fought so hard to keep it. The sheer *normality* of that job helped keep me sane!

"Look, it's *fine!*" I protested. "My ability drains me enough that getting to sleep is not a problem!"

"That sounds *precisely* like a problem!" Sarah shot back. "You're spending all your time either working or trying to survive! When do you get to *live?*"

"I have fun!" I countered. "Sometimes… which reminds me! Earl said he'd have some Project Top Hat work for me tomorrow, so there's that!"

"What's Project Top Hat?" Emily asked, looking like she agreed with Sarah's assessment that I worked too much.

"Oh, I've heard of this!" Sarah announced, sounding excited. "It's with the FBI, isn't it?"

"Yep!" I agreed. "It's using my ability to find lost or missing persons!"

"How did Earl sucker you into doing *that?*" Emily sneered.

"It's my *preferred* type of work, actually…" I huffed.

"Because it lets you save people, right?" Sarah asked, a knowing look on her face.

"Exactly!" I smiled back. "It lets me live out a fantasy of people coming to the rescue, something I had wished for, for so long…"

"*Only you…*" Emily sighed, bowing her head in surrender.

"Humph!" I harrumphed, leading to an awkward silence before we all broke out in giggles.

"Still, though…" Sarah interjected, "I *do* worry about you…"

"I'll be okay," I reassured. "I Just need to get past this thing with Tim, and wait for my leg to heal up, then my life will go back to some semblance of normal, at least normal for *me…*"

"Anyway!" Emily declared loudly, clearly forcing a change of subject. "We've got a room ready for you, so why don't I help you settle in?"

"And I'll get started on dinner!" I announced, getting up.

May you live in interesting times… yeah, when has my life *not* been interesting?

Stupid Chinese curse…

Chapter 10

Life's Tests

Sarah promised to leave us alone the next day by doing the whole tourist thing while Emily and I drove off for the antique shop. Emily would be working retail while I would be down in the bunker taking my Korean proficiency test. I confess I was confident I would do well, largely because I couldn't really do much of anything else while laid up with a broken leg, so I had spent all my time studying.

I inched my way down to the basement, lamenting every step, and went through the rigmarole of getting into the bunker. From there, I took a computerized test that tested how well I read the language, followed by a one-on-one interview with a native speaker. At the end of the test, he smiled and told Earl that I spoke it like a native, which made me blush a little.

"Now, test the connection with this," Earl commanded, handing me a star-shaped medal attached to a bit of ribbon, with a brass pin to hold it in place. It was the kind of medal that's pinned to a soldier's uniform.

I took the medal in my fingertips, relaxed my mind, and started pushing my awareness into it. Immediately, I saw twisted fragments of a long corridor that seemed to stretch endlessly. I looked behind me to see a battalion of monsters wearing American uniforms carrying huge guns and spitting fire. I felt a wave of terror as I ran as fast as I could, only to have the hall in front of me stretch out to infinity while the monsters behind me inched ever closer!

I confess it took me longer than it *should* have to realize I was getting a glimpse of a dream.

"It's a good connection," I commented, placing the medal on the table while trying to shake loose the vision I had seen.

"Good," Earl nodded, looking satisfied, before handing me a digital recorder I had become totally familiar with. "Then you'll start tonight. Report your findings in this and we'll debrief in the mornings, like before."

"Is it okay if I record everything in Korean?" I asked, taking the recorder. "It's just easier not to have to switch mental gears, you know?"

"It's *better* for us if you record it in Korean," Earl agreed. "Gives us better operational security. If it leaks out, they'll assume it's a defector in Korea rather than an American."

"Good," I affirmed, more to let him know that I had heard him than anything else. I had known he'd agree to me recording it this way, since he had before, but it's always better to ask.

Satisfied that all was well on that end, Earl pulled out a large cardboard box from the metal storage closet he kept in the room. He set the box on the table and opened it, revealing a number of smaller plastic bags, each sealed with red evidence tape, with a case file carefully labelled on the outside.

"We've got some Project Top Hat work," Earl informed me, needlessly, like I *hadn't* been waiting for this.

I confess I smiled at this, enjoying the work more than I rightfully *should* have, but this *was* the payoff for all the spy-work he had me do, after all.

The first bag I pulled out held what looked to be a worn-out white t-shirt with the word 'whatever' and some sort of emoticon on it. I opened the bag and got the distinctive whiff of body odor and perfume, which I welcomed as a good sign. My ability works better on clothing that has been well-worn and hasn't been washed, not entirely unlike a bloodhound, come to think of it.

I took a calming breath, took the shirt in my hands, relaxed my mind, and plunged into the head of someone sitting out in the warm rain.

"Spare some change, sir?" a girlish voice asked, holding out a pale hand to a man in a suit pretending not to notice her. I felt the gnawing pains of hunger along with the absolute miserable feeling of being totally alone.

I was in the head of a teenaged runaway girl and for a brief moment, I considered not telling Earl what I was experiencing. I confess my thoughts had drifted to the time *I* had run away, which had forever altered my life for the better. To be fair, though, my father and step-mother had never bothered to report me missing, while *this* girl's parents obviously *had*. They cared enough about her that they had done what was necessary to get her back safely.

For her, it was running away from people that loved her; for me it was *escaping* my *captors.*

I spent some more time with her, trying to glean where she was. I told Earl of the different street names I saw as well as the buildings. I even went so far as to whisper into her head, asking how things had come to this. The story I got was that she had run away with a college boy, who had promised her the world if she only came with him. He took her to 'the big city' and immediately tried to become her pimp. She had recoiled at this, scratched his face up badly, hopefully enough to leave a good scar on the bastard as far as I was concerned. From there, she was too ashamed to face her parents again, and too broke to get out of the city, so she was trying to make it on her own, and failing… badly…

I reported all this to Earl, including the city name and the streets I had seen through her eyes. He got on the phone with the local police and guided them to her location. She resisted at first, the shame overwhelming the two of us, but a little pushing from me and some firm resolve on the officer's part was enough to break her meager defenses.

She would be on her way back home to people that cared about her.

I took a quick breather after that session, sorting out the other bags into the broad categories of hits and misses. There were more misses than hits, but that was par for the course. Many missing-persons are dead within a few days of abduction, and my ability doesn't work on ghosts, at least not in that way. The only two items I managed to get a hit off of were an old diary and a tiny pink shirt, the kind that would only fit a toddler.

Once I had recovered enough, I dove into the head belonging to the tiny pink shirt. Immediately, I was sitting in a restrictive plastic seat in the back of a car. I saw a man in the driver's seat and the word 'daddy' popped into my head. The thoughts I got were largely jumbled and non-verbal but the impression I got was that of a toddler being abducted by her father. In many respects, this case was more challenging than the teenaged runaway since the girl hadn't learned the language yet, but I could still see roads and signs well enough, even if she didn't know what to make of them. As far as she was concerned, she was just going on a trip with her daddy, rather than being kidnapped in a custody dispute.

Once again, I was able to guide Earl to her location, made easier when they stopped at a gas station with an address on the front. A quick look out the car was enough information to relay to highway patrol. Before long, the car had been pulled over by officers who had seen the amber alert along with the tip from Project Top Hat, in the guise of the FBI.

Another happy ending! I basked in the joy of it for several minutes while I caught my breath.

The diary was last and from Earl's expression, was one that made him both concerned and angry. It didn't take me long to understand why. The diary belonged to a soldier that had run away from base, deserting his comrades. The man was scared out of his mind, making his thoughts a rambling mess of both useful and useless information. This one took less time than the others because the military police were already looking for him, and had even tracked him down to the city he was in, but were uncertain *exactly* where he was. With my help, they tracked him down easily and brought him in with nothing but the feeblest excuse for resistance.

It would not end well for him…

Still, even *with* the deserter, it was a good day for Project Top Hat and I was satisfied.

"That does it for me," Earl announced, packing up the rest of the evidence bags back into the box. "Don't forget about tonight!" Earl reminded me as I got up to make my way to the airlock connecting to the basement of the antique store.

"I won't forget," I promised automatically.

I confess I was surprised to see Anne seemingly waiting for me outside the bunker door!

"You done in there for the day?" she asked, looking nervous. Ever since I had told her what the large steel door *really* led to, she seemed to give it a wide berth, like she was afraid she would see something she wasn't supposed to and they'd have to kill her for it.

"All done!" I sang, suppressing a yawn. I'd have to take a nap before I did my spying on North Korea. As much as I love Project Top Hat, it takes a lot out of me!

"Good!" Anne nodded, still eyeing the bunker door with suspicion. "Emily could use your help. I've had her on the register all day and she's getting… *fidgety*… I'd help her out, but I'm heading out to an estate sale."

"I can take over at the register," I volunteered. "Sitting is about all I can do, anyway!"

"Good," Anne sighed in obvious relief. "Thank you so much!"

"No problem!" I smiled before inching my way up the basement steps, with Anne behind me looking both nervous and impatient. I'm guessing she was nervous because she feared I would fall and impatient because stairs have become the bane of my existence as they take *forever* to go up or down in them.

"Hey Emily!" I called as I made my way to the register. "Want me to take over the register while you do the rounds of the store?"

"Hell yes!" she cheered, jumping off the seat and practically leaving a dust trail as she ran off to help customers around the store.

I sighed as I sat down on the stool, setting my crutches against the wall and preparing for dull monotony. Out of something that was increasingly becoming a habit, I opened the special tracker app that Earl had given me to help me keep track of Tim's movements, while also fervently pushing aside thoughts that this made me a stalker. The app showed him just outside the store, which did not bode well. I pulled up the history tab and saw that he'd been out there for more than thirty minutes, which was odd and exceedingly creepy as I wondered if he had been stalking me using less advanced techniques than I had been using to stalk *him.*

Sure enough, I glanced up to see him heading towards the door. I hastily put my phone away, lest he see what I had been using it for, and put on a face that *should* scream 'totally innocent' that I confess I *might* have practiced a bit in the mirror.

"I *know* it was *you!*" he accused angrily shoving a finger in my face.

"What was me?" I asked in my sweetest voice.

"I know you put a virus on my servers!" he declared, his face starting to turn an ugly scarlet.

"You have your own servers?" I wondered aloud, going for completely oblivious.

"I know you know about the article I wrote about you!" he insisted.

"You wrote an article about me?" I echoed, still sounding sweet. "Did you write nice things about me?" I added, knowing I was provoking him, yet still needing to maintain the innocent act.

"You know *damn* well it wasn't!" he shouted, drawing the attention of the other customers.

"Really?" I asked, sounding hurt. "Do you think I could get a copy of that? You know, to make sure you didn't say anything… *libelous* about me?"

At this, Tim's face started to blanche. Yeah, being a journalist, the word 'libel' has some especially important, and terrifying, implications. I had been careful to choose it *just* for him.

"I mean," I added perhaps a little mercilessly, "you *can* back up everything you said about me, right? You didn't make any unsubstantiated claims, *right?"*

Tim's face blanched further and I wondered, somewhat idly, if he would faint.

"You *have* read the article!" he accused.

"Nope!" I sang. "You just told me you said mean things about me and put them in an article! That sounds like something I'd want to read and perhaps give to a lawyer, since you're a 'journalist' and all. That seems fair, doesn't it?"

This left Tim spluttering for a moment, but he recovered himself quickly enough to snarl, "They *will* get you! I'll make *sure* of it!"

"Oh dear…" I chided gently. "Now *that* sounds like a *threat!* That's not good at all…"

Tim stormed out the door, trying to slam it, but the door had one of those hydraulic springs that prevent it from being slammed, which only seemed to frustrate him all the more.

There *was* one part of that conversation that had me on edge, though… He had said that *they* will get you. Who the hell were *they?*

My question looked like it would soon be answered as I saw Tim consulting with a couple of men in suits that seemed to be waiting for him outside the store.

One man was tall and looked like a pale linebacker with a square jaw; the other, while shorter, was still taller than me and looked lanky with curly black hair and cold, confident, eyes. I immediately pegged the shorter man as the more dangerous of the two, based on his confident stance and the way Tim seemed to defer to him more so than the other one.

My mind immediately jumped to the worst-case-scenario and it took all I had not to panic. It's possible that these men *weren't* Prizrak, and were, instead, some con-men looking at Tim like an easy mark, but when have I *ever* been so lucky?

If I was right, and they really *were* Prizrak, the Russian version of Project Aesop, then I was *seriously* screwed!

The men seemed to finish their talk with Tim and turned towards the store, taking the few strides to the front door.

Aw hell and blast and crap on toast!

What the hell am I going to do *now?*

Chapter 11

Prizrak

The two men came into the store and made a beeline for me at the register.

Now that they were in the store, I got a better look at the two of them. The tall linebacker wasn't alone. He was accompanied by three women, all of whom would have been pretty had their throats not been slit from ear to ear. They kept moaning in wet gurgles, with pink foam oozing from their wounds.

I hate ghosts when they're still in their gory phase…

The other one, though, had onyx-black skin, cold, dead eyes, and a confident swagger. Yep, this one was definitely the one in charge. He'd be the first one to speak, I'd bet on it.

"Tell me about the woman living in the mansion," the black man, the shorter of the two, demanded, confirming my prediction. He spoke in something approaching an American accent, but it sounded… slightly off, though I couldn't say exactly how… The more I looked at him, the more familiar he looked, but I still couldn't place him.

"What do you want with her?" I asked, acting innocent to play for time.

"She killed my brother!" the man accused. His taller companion seemed to be hanging back, keeping watch on everyone else.

"Is that so?" I gasped. "I haven't heard of them killing anyone!"

"So you know who she is!" he declared.

"Well, I haven't heard of *any* deaths recently," I pondered. "I mean, there was Mr. Boday, but he was killed by the Cryptic Killer, who was a *man,* not a woman…"

"That's not him!" he snarled, getting frustrated.

"Well, I haven't heard of anyone else dying, much less *murdered!"* I retorted.

"He disappeared after going to her place!" he asserted.

"Wait, I'm confused…" I mumbled. "First you say he was *murdered,* and now you say he *disappeared?"*

"They are the *same!"* he insisted.

"They really are *not* the same," I shot back. "Maybe he just doesn't want to speak to you."

"He would not *do* that!" he snarled.

"How can you be so sure?" I asked, as innocently as I could, still trying to place why the hell he looked so familiar.

"Because I'm his *brother!*" he shouted. I was fully aware that my ignorance act was pissing him off something awful, but I didn't see an alternative that didn't make me a *bigger* target than I already was with him!

"Let's try something else," I sighed. "What do you know about this woman who you say killed your brother when, really, you just can't find him."

"She's a black woman," he told me.

I waited for him to continue, but when he didn't, I prompted, "And?"

"And she killed him!"

"Look," I sighed, feeling like we weren't getting anywhere, "I don't know of any black woman living in a mansion around here," I told him flat-out.

Wait… if he was looking for a black woman in a mansion *and* he might be Prizrak, then he might mean he's looking for Sha-De, who used to be my live-in nurse, and if *that's* the case, then his brother might be the Black Scorpion!

Aw, hell and blast!

"Journalist says you *do!*" he insisted, jabbing a finger at me.

"Yeah, well, he also says the pyramids were built by *aliens,*" I snarked back at him with a weary sigh. "So, maybe you shouldn't believe everything he says about me…"

"Jane? What's going on?" came Emily's voice from the stairs. "Is everything okay?"

"This man says he's looking for a black woman that lives in a mansion around here," I told her as calmly as I could.

"What black woman?" she asked, looking confused.

"Not sure," I lied. "He seems to think she killed his brother, but he also says that his brother just disappeared!"

"Wait, so which is it?" she asked, looking more confused than ever.

"Gah!" the man screamed in frustration, making a few other customers turn to watch the free show going on in front of them.

"Sir," I told him sternly, "I am going to have to ask you to *leave!* You are disturbing our other customers!"

"Tell me about Agent Dreamer!" he demanded. "The journalist says you know them!"

"I don't know who you're talking about," I lied. "Now, please leave!"

"I *know* you're lying!" he insisted, his fake accent slipping, sounding more Eastern European. "Journalist says you and Dreamer are in same places at same time!"

"The only Dreamer I know," I confessed, "works for the corporate company that owns this store. She took me on a trip one time to help find some new merchandise for the store, like these," I motioned to a stand holding pendants featuring the veves of several of the more popular Loa in Voodooan culture. The pendants were large, about the size of a half-dollar, and were gold-colored metal inscribed with a symbol of the Loa they represented. The one I wore around my neck was a gift from Sha-Do, Voodoo Mambo and sister of Sha-De. The one I wore was the veve of Ezili Danto, Loa of motherhood and doing whatever is necessary to protect children. The symbol on mine looked like a frilly Valentine's day heart surrounded by crosses and pierced by three large daggers. Personally, I didn't believe in the Loa, but I *did* believe in valuing a gift given to me by someone I considered a friend.

"These pendants," I continued, "are the veves, or personal symbols, of the Loa, or powerful spirits."

"I do not *care* about *trinkets!*" he shouted angrily, his accent now *screaming* Russian. "Tell me about this Dreamer!"

"She works for *corporate,*" I insisted. "She's *not* an agent of any kind!" I continued the lie.

"Tell me how to contact her," he commanded, his voice going cold.

"I don't know," I told him just as coldly. "I'm just a *cashier*. I don't *know* how to contact corporate. They mostly leave this store alone."

The man tried to reach for me, but I leaned back, and would have *run* if I had been able to. Instead, I reached for my phone and pretended to dial the sheriff.

"Sheriff?" I panted into the phone. "There are some men here that are threatening me at the store! I've asked them to leave, but one of them just tried to *grab* me!"

The man scowled at me before turning around in a huff, heading back outside to Tim Foyle. I saw some gruff words exchanged, but didn't catch anything other than raised voices and hostile body language.

"Who were they?" Emily asked, coming to my side.

"Trouble," I answered, grimly. "We need to tell Earl about this. Now! Go find anyone still in the store and bustle them out. Make up something. We're closing for a while."

"You gonna wait here for the sheriff?" she asked, her face screwing up in concentration.

"Didn't actually call her," I whispered, not wanting anyone else to overhear.

"What? Why not?" she hissed.

"Well, for one thing, I'm pretty sure the taller of the two is a trained killer," I told her, going for nonchalantly, "and for another thing, I'm *certain* that those men are Prizrak."

"How can you be sure?" she asked, sounding nervous.

"Ghosts for the killer and I figured out who the brother is, that he spoke of," I answered. "If I'm right, and I'm damned sure that I am, bringing the sheriff here would have escalated the situation beyond what we could handle. I'll let Earl decide whether to bring the sheriff in on this, but for now, we need more information."

"Right," she nodded before heading off to the rest of the store.

I wondered, idly, what excuse she would give the customers. It would need to be major enough to warrant closing the store, but also minor enough that it wouldn't cause a stir with police.

I know, I know… the lie that she told people is a minor issue, compared to the *major* issue of having a couple of Prizrak agents in the same *state,* much less the same *town* that I was in, but I was having trouble processing the enormity of the *shit* I was in at the moment, so it served as a useful distraction.

Dammit Tim Foyle!

Chapter 12

War Council

"That's the last of them," Emily informed me as she bustled two men out the door.

"Good," I decided as I locked the door, then led the way downstairs.

"You know," Emily commented, "this would be easier if *I* was given access to the bunker…"

"Take it up with Earl," I retorted with a small huff as I inched my way down another step. I cannot *tell* you how happy I'll be once I'm rid of these damned crutches. Hell and blast, I was supposed to be taking it *easy,* while at *home,* not going up and down too damned many stairs all day long!

We got to the door and I swiped my access card, activated my key fob, put in the code for the door, before placing my thumb in the area indicated on the screen. After that, we were in the airlock and the two of us dumped our phones in the little cubbyhole boxes set into the wall. The last lock was a retina scanner which opened the door to the inner chamber, where I saw Earl watching the monitors, including the one right outside the doors…

The bastard had probably watched the whole lengthy procedure of getting in here and hadn't lifted a *finger* to help by opening the outer door to see what the hell was the matter!

"Problem?" he asked, sounding innocent.

"Did you see them?" I asked, making my way to the only other seat in the room and slumping down, panting a little.

"Belligerent customers?" he asked, still not seeing the issue.

"Prizrak," I declared, staring him down.

"Are you sure?" he demanded, his tone *finally* turning serious.

"As sure as I *can* be," I told him. "I'm pretty sure the one I was talking to is the brother to Black Scorpion."

"Remind me, who's Black Scorpion?" Emily asked, sounding concerned, but not overly so.

"He's a screamer that was putting our people in comas," Earl explained.

"What happened to him?" she followed-up.

"I happened," I sighed. When her face told me she was expecting more, I continued, "It was right after I got out of the hospital from the Chicago incident. He thought he was coming after Sha-De, my live-in nurse, but she was gone by then. The kids bloodied him up a bit, and I used the blood to get into his head and gave him some horrible memories."

"And now he has to be strapped down and heavily sedated at night," Earl informed us.

"Really?" Emily asked, looking shocked, before turning to me with a little fear in her eyes.

"I've got Mr. Fluffybutt and therapy to help me," I told her, waving off her fear of me.

"Do they know who you are?" Earl asked me point-blank.

"Not yet," I sighed. "They only know what Tim told them, so they think I'm connected to Agent Dreamer. I'm pretty sure they're either looking for her or Sha-De and only see me as a possible connection to Dreamer."

"What did you tell them about Dreamer?" he asked, his face turning into a mostly unreadable mask.

"That the only Dreamer I knew worked for corporate and that I knew nothing about her being an agent of *any* kind," I explained in as professional a tone as I could muster.

"Always good to keep lies consistent," Earl smiled, making me roll my eyes. Please, as if I didn't *already* know that!

"So, what do we do *now?"* Emily asked, sounding stressed.

"The agents are the immediate problem," Earl evaded.

"But Tim is the root problem," I countered.

"Agreed," Earl sighed. "I'll call in reinforcements to surveil the agents, maybe see where they're staying. If we're lucky, we can grab something of theirs…"

"And then I can keep an eye on them," I agreed.

"Right," Earl nodded. "Now, do you know if either of them are psychic?"

"I didn't feel anything, but if they were sensitives, then there's no guarantee I *would,"* I mused aloud. "One of them is definitely a hit-man, though. One that prefers slitting throats."

"How can you be sure?" Earl asked, looking like he already knew the answer.

"Three ghosts still in their gory phase," I answered as nonchalantly as I could. "All were women, all were pissed."

"Gory phase?" Emily asked, looking like she immediately regretted asking the question.

"New ghosts tend to look like how they died," I explained, my tone turning professorial. "Once they realize that they're dead and operate under different rules, they tend to look like everybody else."

"So… you *saw*…" she hesitated, looking squeamish.

"Three bloodless women with their throats slit, yeah…" I finished for her.

"I'm living in a goddam *horror* movie!" Emily muttered under her breath.

"Welcome to my world," I sighed. "Just be glad you don't have to *see* them! At least these three were fairly mild, though their gurgles were unsettling…"

Emily looked close to *screaming!* She *really* does not like ghost stories! I regretted mentioning how they sounded, after seeing the terror on her face.

"Look, I'm sorry, okay?" I apologized, albeit badly. "I guess I've just gotten *used* to seeing the gory dead. I didn't think you'd freak out so badly just from a description of them…"

"I freaking *hate* ghosts!" Emily muttered, obviously tuning us out.

"So, what do we do about *Tim?*" I asked, trying to get us back on track.

"I was thinking of sending Agent Dreamer," Earl smirked.

"You're *not* serious!" I gasped, looking pointedly at my crutches.

"Dreamer is just an *alias,*" Earl explained, shooting a glance at Emily. "It doesn't have to be *you!*"

Okay, I confess, I can be a bit slow at times, but I managed to catch his meaning, eventually.

"She's got the right hair for it," I commented, looking Emily over. "All she needs are the sunglasses and a coffee cup…"

"Not to mention a suit," Earl added.

"Maybe a little makeup, and a whole *lot* of attitude!" I smiled, liking this idea more and more.

"Why do I feel like a cow at auction?" Emily muttered, giving the both of us the evil eye.

"Think of it as serving your country!" Earl rebuked a little mercilessly.

"I can walk you through it," I cajoled. "It'll be easier since Tim has never met Dreamer. All you *really* have to focus on will be her attitude."

"And what *is* her attitude?" she asked warily.

"One of utter contempt for anyone that isn't her," Earl answered before I had a chance to.

Emily turned to me for confirmation, so I gave it to her with a quick, "Pretty much!"

"Okay," Emily sighed dejectedly. "So, the plan is to… what? Go scare Tim into giving up his plan to work for people he *thinks* are working for the US government?"

"And to show him just how deep in the shit he really is!" Earl added with determined vehemence.

"Should we also tell him that the people he's working with are really Russians?" I asked, considering the implications of this.

"And maybe win him over to our side?" Earl considered. "Might not be a bad idea!"

As far as plans go, it was kinda half-assed, but we were dealing with a bit of a time-crunch and we didn't have a whole lot to work with, so we tried to make do as best we could.

Besides, haven't you ever noticed that the more meticulously you plan something, the more likely it is to go off the rails?

Story of my life…

Chapter 13

Acting Lessons

"Okay, so walk me through this again," Emily sighed dramatically. "What do I need to pull this off?"

"Well, you need a suit," I told her, checking off things on my fingers, "some large sunglasses, a coffee cup, a bit of makeup, and a whole lotta attitude."

"Well, I've got the suit, and I suppose we could stop for coffee…" Emily hesitated, maybe not too clear on the character. "But, what do you mean about my makeup?"

"Just some work to make it look like you have cheekbones," I judged aloud, critiquing her round, babyish, face. "And you can borrow my sunglasses. Good news is you've already got the hair, so you won't need a wig!"

"How reassuring…" she scowled. "Okay, so what is her background?"

"Well, she's about ten years older than me," I started, thinking aloud.

"Wait!" she demanded. "She's *older* than you? And you can pull that off?"

"She does," Earl agreed. "Easily."

Emily just huffed at this.

"And as far as her attitude goes," I continued. "Think of her as someone that holds everyone else in utter contempt and doesn't care that they hate her for it."

"Wow!" Emily proclaimed. "She sounds like a total *bitch!*"

"Exactly!" I smirked. "*Embrace* the bitch! *Be* the bitch!"

"Okay, who came up with this character?" she asked, sounding somewhat exasperated. "Normally, an alias is one that *doesn't* get noticed!"

"Except that Dreamer's purpose is to get everyone to leave her the hell *alone,* and being a cold-hearted bitch does the job nicely," Earl intoned.

"I've always found it liberating!" I added somewhat cheerfully.

"You *would!*" she sneered.

"What do you mean?" I asked, fairly confused and a little offended.

"You're always so quiet, and you mostly go along with what everyone else wants," she answered, with a strong dose of pity in her voice. "You're practically a *doormat!*"

"Well…" I muttered quietly. "I grew up in a house where talking back meant more whippings…"

"Right, crappy childhood…" she sighed. "I keep forgetting…"

"So, about the attitude…" I suggested, trying to get things back on track.

"Right, arrogant contempt, I think I can manage that!" she affirmed. "Now, is she this way to *everyone,* or…"

"Only to people that she doesn't think are useful," I finished for her. "For example, she worked with a Mambo in New Orleans to catch the Locked Room Killer."

"And there's always Agent Max Flagg," Earl added, unhelpfully.

"Max Flagg?" Emily asked, suspiciously.

"Meaning Earl," I answered before Earl could say anything.

"Right! I figured as much…" she sighed. "Okay, so what's the plan, then? I go to Tim as Agent Dreamer, then do my best to intimidate the hell out of him, then try to get him onto our side?"

"That's about it," Earl nodded. "I'll escort you as Agent Max Flagg. Two agents are bound to be more intimidating than one!"

"And I can be in your head for support," I added, not totally liking the idea of someone playing a part I created.

"I *guess*…" she sighed, looking like she didn't like this idea one bit. To be fair, though, I'm pretty sure all her other work as an agent was more behind the scenes and she did her best *not* to get noticed, whereas Dreamer's job was to be front-and-center, taking charge of whatever mess she was handed.

"You ladies should get back to Jane's place," Earl instructed, "get into character, and I'll come by to pick up Agent Dreamer to head over to Tim's place."

"What about Anne?" Emily asked, possibly stalling for time.

"Anne should be back soon," I thought aloud. "Estate sales don't usually take up a lot of time, unless she's buying in bulk to wrangle a discount. Even then, we can afford to wait until after she gets back, right?"

"Waiting might be useful," Earl mused, quietly. "It would give Foyle time to finish up with the agents he's working with. I'd prefer holding off confronting them if we can..."

"Then it's settled," I declared. "We'll wait for Anne to get back, then head back to my place to get Emily suited up and in character, you'll pick her up, and I'll play support."

Earl nodded his head in agreement. Emily... looked less sure of the plan...

We left the bunker and Emily took the lead heading back upstairs, leaving me to follow after her, cursing every step. I swear I'll *never* complain about having to take the stairs again, once my leg heals up!

By the time I got back upstairs, Emily had unlocked the front door and flipped the sign back to show that we were open. Once I was firmly entrenched at the cash register, Emily left to do the rounds of the store, I guess to make sure products were in their place on the shelves or something, since there wasn't anybody in the store...

An hour or two later, Anne came back carrying several large cardboard boxes.

"Good haul at the estate sale?" I asked, wondering just how heavy the boxes were.

"They had a bunch of old books that they were just planning to *throw out!"* she practically squealed. "Can you *believe* it?"

"Hard to imagine," I conceded, trying to think of a good way to bring up Emily and I having to leave to prepare a confrontation with Tim.

"So, um..." I hesitated, biting my lip. "Something came up and Emily and I have to leave to take care of it... Is it okay if we leave now? I can help with those items tomorrow, if you need me, but not today..."

"What's wrong?" Anne asked, sounding a little alarmed.

"Tim is causing trouble..." I answered cautiously, afraid of going too far. "He's done something and now we're all kind of... in over our heads..."

"Are you in danger?" Anne asked, sounding more alarmed.

"Maybe," I shrugged, trying to shake off her concern. "But we have a plan!"

"Anything I can do to help?" she asked, setting the boxes down, looking ready to spring into action.

"If you see Tim," I considered, "maybe call the sheriff… Tim may not realize it, but he's in more danger than he thinks…"

"Alright," she nodded, taking me totally seriously. "If you and Emily need to take off, you go right ahead. I can manage the store the rest of the day."

"Thank you so much!" I sighed in relief, still a little worried that I had revealed too much.

Emily must have heard me talking in the quiet store because she was just coming down the stairs as Anne was telling me she was just going to drop off the boxes downstairs before coming back to man the register.

"We good to go?" Emily asked, looking towards Anne's retreating form.

"As soon as Anne comes back upstairs," I agreed.

"Good," she sighed, a little nervously.

"You'll be *fine,*" I reassured her. "Remember, if it all goes to hell, *I'm* the one in deadly danger!"

"And yet you seem so much *calmer* than I am!" she whined.

"Only on the outside," I assured her. "I'm panicking so bad, I'm not sure I could *eat!*"

Emily snickered at this, which turned into a full-blown chuckle when she saw how deadly serious I was…

Humph!

Emily drove us back to my place, with Peter opening the gate for us.

"Automatic gate… automatic gate…" Emily mumbled to herself. Whatever helps her cope, I guess…

Back at the house, I saw Sarah sweeping the first floor.

Aw, hell and blast! I forgot about her!

"Sarah!" I called. "You really don't have to clean!"

"But I *want* to!" she insisted. "I know you can't do it yourself in your condition, so I thought I might as well make myself useful!"

Emily gave me a look that was part panic and part suggestion.

"Sarah," I sighed, seeing no way around this. "There's something I have to tell you, that I'm honestly not sure I'm *allowed* to tell you, so you *have* to keep it a secret, okay?"

Sarah stopped her sweeping and gave me her full attention, waiting for me to continue.

"I have an alias with the FBI" I plunged into my explanation. "Her name is Agent Dreamer. Because of what Tim did, *Emily* will be playing the part of Dreamer this afternoon."

Emily waved at the mention of her name before running up the stairs, presumably to put her suit on.

"I'm going to be staying here providing support," I continued. "But you should know, there are Russian agents in town."

"Are they after you?" she asked, her face turning pale.

"They are, but they don't *realize* it yet," I sighed. "Right now, they just think I might be *friends* with Agent Dreamer. So far, I don't think they've made any connection to Nightmare and we're working to *keep* it that way. Earl will be calling in reinforcements to monitor the agents, but in the meantime, I need you to stay in the house, okay?"

"But what can we do if they come here?" she asked, eyeing the door and the furnishings, perhaps looking for makeshift weapons.

"Kids!" I called out to the house at large, bringing Peter and Wendy flying into the room to hover in front of me.

"Kids," I began again, addressing the two of them. "There are some Russian agents that are after me."

"Oh no!" Wendy cried, looking fearful.

"I'll get them!" Peter declared, looking determined.

I nodded approval at Peter and continued, "One is a large man with three other ghosts anchored to him. They're still in their gory phase. You'll recognize them because it's three women whose throats have been slit. The other is a black man that's the brother of the Black Scorpion. You remember him?"

"He's the one that came looking for you," Wendy answered.

"We showed *him!"* Peter enthused.

"Right!" I agreed. "Now, if you see *either* of those men…" I paused, considering my words carefully. There are times that call for subtlety and there are times where subtlety should be thrown out the window. If these men ever found out who I *really* was, they'd show me no mercy. Because of this, I figured subtlety would be a liability, rather than an asset. "If you see them," I began again, "show them no mercy."

"You got it!" the two of them cheered enthusiastically before flying off to search the perimeter.

"When you told them to 'show no mercy' how will they take that?" Sarah asked, looking a little pale.

"The kids will use lethal force to defend me," I answered immediately, certain of my answer even as my voice turned cold. "Ghosts don't view life and death the same way we do. As far as Peter and Wendy are concerned, there's little difference."

"Then why haven't they killed you?" Sarah asked in a somewhat creepy voice.

"Because there's no guarantee that I would make a ghost," I answered matter-of-factly. "Or if I did, there's no guarantee that I'd anchor to the house. If I'm gone, I can't make them stronger and I can't play with them. Then there's the possibility that whoever ends up buying the house would tear it down, which would probably destroy them in the process."

"I'd find that interesting if we weren't talking life-and-death…" Sarah muttered, looking a little shaken.

I shrugged off her concern before making my way to the basement stairs. "I've got to get Dreamer's ID and badge," I explained to her over my shoulder.

Great… *more* stairs… stupid crutches… stupid cultist… stupid brainwashed cop…

My basement is probably one of the creepier places I've seen, or at least it *would* be if I got creeped out by harsh shadows, cobwebs everywhere, and several large spiders not bothering to hide.

I confess I always thought it weird how worked up people get over spiders. Personally, I've always *liked* spiders. For one thing, spiders don't hunt humans, so they tend to either run from us or leave us alone. For another, spiders take out some of the pests around here, especially mosquitoes! I *hate* the nasty flying bloodsuckers! I barely have enough blood for *me,* let alone some parasitic flying insect!

I moved across the concrete floor, seeing games of tic-tac-toe played in the dust, without any sign of anyone stepping up to them. I maneuvered past the empty shelves placed here from previous owners who didn't want to come back to the haunted house to collect them, and finally to the back of the stairs, whose view is blocked off by several more shelves. I grabbed the flashlight I keep on a nearby shelf and shine it on a vent set into the wall. It's a false vent, with a black felt background, that hides a safe I had installed while I was fixing up the rest of the house.

I tug on the vent, pulling out and up, and it slides up on spring-assisted hinges above the hole holding the safe. I punch in the nine-digit code, I change every week, and the lock disengages with a thunk that seems loud in the small space. I turned the handle and open the door, revealing two small shelves holding knickknacks that no thief would think was really valuable. Among the items are a five-year sobriety coin given to me by Dr. Teddy Bear, a pack of playing cards, several IDs, and a silver lighter given to me by Monet Baggs, a friend that helped me out during the last mission.

They may not have much value on their own, but for me, they were keys into the minds of people that trusted me and that I confidently called my friends.

I grabbed the deck of cards along with the ID and badge and stuck them in a pocket before closing up the safe and setting the vent back in place. By the time I got back upstairs, Emily was already wearing her black suit that screamed 'government agent' which I approved of, until I saw a noticeable bulge on the left side of her chest.

"Agent Dreamer doesn't use a gun," I announced, coming to a stop in front of Emily and Sarah.

"She's an FBI agent," Emily declared, indignantly. "Of *course* she has a gun!"

"She's never had a gun *before!*" I protested.

"Does Tim know that?" she inquired, quirking her eyebrows.

"Please don't make this a thing…" I whined.

"Jane…" Sarah chided gently, "just because *you* don't use a gun, doesn't mean that *she* can't use a gun. If she's facing off against Russian agents, she'll be more believable if she has a gun."

I sighed in defeat before digging out Dreamer's ID and badge, handing them over to Emily without further protest.

"Can I borrow something of yours?" I asked. "Something that's emotionally significant to you."

"For your ability, right?" she asked, looking hesitant.

"Right," I nodded.

Emily looked pensive for a moment, biting her lip, like she was considering whether or not to trust me with something so valuable to her. Finally, she sighed and dug out a keychain that looked to be a worn piece of clear plastic with little stars embedded in it.

"Do *not* lose this," she warned, the threat clear in her voice.

"I'll keep it safe for you," I promised. I held the little keychain in my fingertips, testing the connection, which was… *strong!* Like, *handshake* strong! I tested it further, making sure it connected to *her* mind and not somebody else's.

I learned *that* lesson the *really* hard way!

What I saw when my mind connected was a rather frail-looking girl wearing a cast that almost looked as heavy as she was, with her face screwed up in concentration, while her eyes had a distant, glazed, look about them.

'She better not lose that!' Emily's thoughts came quick and heated.

'I promise I'll keep it safe,' I sent to her, making her jump with a little shriek.

"Oh, you'll have to school your face better than *that!'* Sarah chided with a little chuckle.

Emily just looked at her, wide-eyed, her face practically screaming *'How?'*

"It's a little disconcerting to have her voice in your head, isn't it?" Sarah asked, knowingly. "I take it that works for you, dear?" she asked, turning to me.

"Best connection I've gotten on an object that wasn't blood!" I commented admiringly. "All the more reason I'll protect it," I promised again, putting it in a pocket of its own.

Emily looked reasonably satisfied at my appraisal, as she let out a small sigh of relief.

"Now for the sunglasses…" I declared, changing the topic.

"I've got them!" Wendy called, carrying them as she flew down the stairs.

Emily screamed and nearly slammed into the wall and I confess I had to work damned hard to keep from chuckling at her fear.

"Thank you, Wendy," I smiled, taking the sunglasses from her and offering them to Emily.

"I will *never* get used to that!" Emily muttered, taking the proffered spectacles.

"It probably helps that I can see them," I shrugged.

"It *might* help," she almost hissed, "until I encountered one of those *gory* ghosts you spoke of! I don't even want to *know* the kinds of scary shit you've seen!"

I shrugged off her concern with a 'what can you do' expression.

You know, if I was a sadistic person, I'd tell her about a ghost that was anchored to some unknown object at the antique store. I'd taken to calling the ghost 'Mr. Roadkill' because of how he looked. He was a motorcyclist, based on his leather coat and partially intact helmet. He was missing his lower jaw, but somehow still had his tongue. Half his face had been scraped clean of flesh and his helmet had been broken through, revealing parts of his skull, with bits of flesh hanging off here and there. He had only communicated in wet, huffing, gurgles, while staring at me with his one remaining eye out of a broken visor.

Yeah, probably better if I *don't* tell her about him…

Once she had the sunglasses on, I noticed that she had already done some makeup work, adding color to define cheekbones, along with a more neutral shade of lipstick. I confess I was kind of jealous. Emily was obviously better at it than I was… Just one of the things I missed out on growing up the way I did…

"So? How do I look?" she asked after a moment.

"You've got the look," I conceded. "Now, can you do the attitude?"

"Pfft!" she snorted, derisively.

"Good!" I encouraged. "But think, more casual indifferent arrogance, and imagine you're holding a coffee cup with your arms crossed."

Emily did as directed, taking her right elbow in her left hand and pretending to hold a paper cup of coffee, her face scowling slightly.

"That'll work!" I nodded appreciatively.

Sarah was giving me an odd look, like she barely recognized me.

"What?" I asked, squirming a little under her gaze.

"Nothing!" she smirked. "I was just thinking that Dreamer might be your real face while this innocent little Jane might be the act!"

I scowled at her in response, not knowing what to say. Emily just smirked, either as part of her act or because she was *really* getting into the role.

"Earl is here!" Peter announced, saving me from having to answer.

"Earl is here," I repeated for everyone else.

"I'll get the door," Emily asserted.

Earl came in holding a cup of coffee, offering it to Emily, who took it, gave it a whiff, then scowled in distaste. Guessing Earl got whatever was cheapest, considering it was just going to be used as a prop.

Earl gave Emily an obvious looking-over and nodded in approval.

"You got the cards?" he asked me.

"Right here," I answered, pulling out the deck of cards.

"What are those for?" Emily asked, looking dubious.

"The cards with the hearts on them," Earl explained, looking like he was in his element, "are printed from ink with my blood mixed in."

"Ew!" Emily winced. "Gross!" she added for good measure.

"They let Jane get in touch with me," Earl replied. "Blood is more reliable than mementos."

"The cards are also less obtrusive," I added. "They helped during the last job."

"You mean the one where you got shot," Emily argued.

"Yes, *that* one," I sighed, somewhat sarcastically. Honestly, did she think I *forgot* that I got *shot?* Even if I *had,* the crutches and cast are pretty big freaking reminders, aren't they?

"You got something from Emily?" Earl asked, either missing or ignoring the little drama between me and Emily.

I held up the keychain that Emily had entrusted me with and added, "I've already tested it. It's got a super-strong connection."

"Good," Earl declared, nodding in satisfaction.

"So, we have our strategy, right?" Emily asked, looking like she was trying to calm her nerves.

"Dreamer is there to run the show," Earl explained confidently. "Flagg is there as backup. We'll tell him that the agents he's working with are really Russian agents and if he doesn't cooperate with us, then we'll charge him with treason."

"And maybe throw in that the girl, *me*, he sicced them on is really just an innocent bystander!" I threw out there, hoping to mitigate any future trouble I had with Tim.

"Right!" Earl agreed. "Jane is on standby, monitoring both of us through the focal objects. If things go fubar, watch for my lead."

"Okay, I've got it," Emily assured. "I'm ready."

"Good! Then let's go," Earl decided, heading back out the front door, while I made my way to the dining room, ready to play spy on the two of them.

Honestly? I was just grateful to get off my feet!

If only sore feet were my biggest problems this day…

Chapter 14

Intimidation

"For the record," Emily intoned, "I don't even *like* coffee!"

'Tough,' I sent to her through the keychain I held in my hand while Sarah tried not to look creepy staring at me as she sat at the seat across from me.

"Then don't drink it," Earl remarked, as he drove down the main street at a sedate pace.

'Now might be a good time to practice talking to me without using your voice,' I suggested to Emily. Talking to people using my ability without actually speaking is one of the more useful skills I've developed. It allows me to hold conversations with people without anyone else knowing about it.

"How do I do that?" Emily demanded out loud.

"Do what?" Earl asked. *"Not* drink coffee?"

"No, sorry," Emily apologized, a little flustered. "Jane is talking into my head and says I should try talking to her without talking out loud."

"Ah!" Earl chuckled. "There's no real trick to it, just think out loud."

Mind you, this is a weird thing to hear from a man that never mastered it…

"Think out loud?" Emily questioned.

'Or think loudly,' I suggested.

"Um…" she mused. *'Like this?'* she sent.

'Good!' I encouraged. *'Just like that!'*

'This feels weird…' she retorted.

'You get used to it,' I assured.

"We're coming up on his house," Earl warned, pulling up to a two-story house that has seen better days.

The house looked like it was an older house, possibly one of the first houses built in the small town. The predominant color was an off-white beige, but there were splotches along the sides that looked like they were amateur repair work that was done using paint that was *close* but not *quite* the same color as the original paint. Several small windows near the base of the house alluded to there being a basement, which only went to figure as nearly *every* house in the Midwest has a basement built to withstand tornadoes.

Earl got out first, with Emily, as Dreamer, right behind. They marched up to the door, which had an actual door-knocker on it and more locks than I could count at first glance, and readied themselves for what was to come. Earl rang the doorbell, pounded on the door, and shouted, "FBI! OPEN UP!"

There was a long pause after him banging on the door, and I briefly checked my app to make sure Tim was still at home, before Emily finally heard muffled sounds of activity inside.

"This is Agent Dreamer with the FBI!" she shouted angrily, her tone one of clear annoyance, for which I was a little proud.

Almost immediately after that, there were sounds of numerous locks being undone before the door opened a crack, several chains securing it to the frame. One of Tim's eyes poked out from the crack, his face well above Emily's eye-level.

"Who are you?" he demanded angrily.

"I'm Agent Dreamer and this is Agent Flagg," Emily announced authoritatively. "We're with the FBI!"

"Show me your badges!" he commanded.

Acting like this was routine, both Earl and Emily dug out their IDs with their aliases on them, and dutifully showed them to Tim.

"What do you want?" he asked, doing his best to sound assertive and mostly succeeding.

Earl glanced at Emily and nodded encouragement, letting her take the lead.

"We want to ask you about the agents you were seen with this morning," she stated, her voice going cold.

"I don't know anything about any agents!" Tim refuted, his voice rising a little in stress.

"May we come inside?" Earl asked in a menacing voice.

"You can talk right there!" Tim insisted.

"That's your choice," Emily intoned in a voice that made it clear she thought it was the *dumbest* choice she could imagine anyone making. "But you might not want your neighbors hearing that you've been aiding and abetting *foreign* agents!"

"They're *not* foreign agents!" Tim countered. "They're CIA agents!"

Earl snorted and I placed a finger on the king of hearts in front of me to get a better idea of what was in his head.

'If there were any other CIA agents in town, I'd know about it!' Earl thought derisively.

'Earl says if they were CIA, he'd know about it,' I passed onto Emily.

'Clearly a ruse,' Emily agreed.

'Tell him you've been tracking the Russian agents,' I suggested into her head.

"I thought you didn't *know* anything about any agents!" Earl quipped a little sarcastically.

"We have reason to believe that they are not *real* CIA agents," Emily warned. "We've been tracking a pair of Russian agents looking to recruit new assets."

"But they showed me their badges!" Tim whined.

"So you *do* know them!" Emily smirked. "If that's the case, would you like to discuss your possible treason *here*, or *downtown*?"

'Tim looks resolute,' I warned Emily. *'Now might be a good time to nudge him a little…'*

Emily took my advice and focused on feelings of intimidation and fear, pushing them outward, while also narrowing the field so that only Tim was affected. I could tell when Tim felt it because his eye went wide and he started undoing the chains holding the door with shaking hands.

"Good choice," Emily encouraged once the door was open and Tim had stepped aside to let them pass.

Earl and Emily wasted no time getting inside and surveying the room they found themselves in. The room was what Emily thought of as 'bachelor messy' as she looked about. With a fair amount of disgust on her part, she saw that the carpet looked like it had never even *seen* a vacuum, there were bits of paper and post-it notes strewn about, and the leather couch had an obvious indent showing where Tim spent much of his time, opposite a big-screen TV mounted on the wall. The few shelves and cupboards had a noticeable layer of dust that would take at least a couple rounds of cleaning to clear up.

From the main room, Emily saw an open doorway that looked like it led to a small kitchen on the other end of the room. There were a set of stairs leading up to the second floor alongside a hallway that probably led to a garage or bathroom, or maybe had basement access. Emily couldn't see down the hall very well as what little light came through the curtains covering the front windows didn't penetrate that far.

Emily's mental image of what she imagined the rest of the house looked like did *not* do Tim any favors...

I confess that, given the mess she had left in my kitchen, I almost laughed at how judgmental she was about *other* people's cleaning habits, or lack thereof... Thankfully, I didn't let this *particular* thought reach her. No sense making her resent me even more than she did already.

"Tell us what you know about the agents you were seen with this morning," Emily demanded in as authoritative a tone as she could manage.

"I *told* you!" Tim snarled. *"They* are not the Russians! *Jane* is!"

Emily snorted contempt at him, asking him, "Jane, the *retail* worker?"

"She's a Russian sleeper agent!" Tim insisted.

"No, she's *not,"* Emily intoned, decisively. "We've already looked into her background," she added for good measure, probably hoping to wrap this up quickly.

"Her *background* is a *sham!"* Tim expostulated. "What the hell even *is* her background? I'll tell you what! She grew up in Russia, then came here under an *obviously* fake name, and bullied her way into the antique shop to serve as *cover* for her going abroad!"

'Aw, hell and blast! I did not bully my way into the shop!' I huffed into Emily's head. *'It was Beth that did that!'*

"Like I said," Emily warned, "we did a full background check on the girl. She came up clean."

"Not that any of that *matters,"* Earl scoffed. *"She's* not the one working with phony CIA agents."

"They are *not* phony!" Tim snarled. "I *saw* their badges!"

"And badges can't be faked?" Emily shot back. "Tell us where they are!"

"Right here!" came a voice from the doorway at the other end of the room. The voice preceded the slender black man holding a gun pointed at Emily and I could feel her heart start to race.

Instinctively, Emily focused on a feeling of peace and nonviolence, pushing it out to the rest of the room. She didn't try to focus it like before, instead letting it radiate out from her in an effort to deescalate the situation.

"So, you can manipulate emotions!" the man asserted, his voice turning to a thick Russian accent. "That must mean you're with Aesop!"

Aw hell and blast! *'He's a sensitive!'* I shouted into Emily's head unnecessarily, earning me a well-earned feeling of sheer annoyance from her.

"What's Aesop?" Tim asked, now looking more confused than ever.

"The more important question," the Russian man intoned, "is who is speaking into your head?"

Oh, *better* and *better*!

I confess I might have started panicking at this pronouncement as Sarah asked, from somewhere far away from directly in front of me, "Jane, are you okay?"

"Prizrak," Earl and I muttered with a scowl on both our faces.

"What the hell is going on here?" Tim demanded, though to be honest, nobody was really paying him any attention by that point.

I mean, he *had* just become the *least* important person in the room, after all…

Crap! *Now* what are we to do?

Chapter 15

Getaway

"Thank you, Mr. Foyle," the leader of the Russians announced in a thick Russian accent, his voice nothing but sincerity. "You have helped us more than we thought possible!"

"But you said you were CIA!" Tim screamed angrily at the man.

"Naturally," the man purred, his face that of a predator that has sighted his prey. "It is easy deception, especially when you would not recognize a *real* ID."

"And what about *you?*" Tim demanded. "Are you the *real* FBI?"

'Maintain the lie,' I intoned in Emily's head.

"Of *course*," Emily huffed, keeping her eye on the two foreign agents.

"Tell me, miss agent," the Russian sneered. "Is the one speaking to you the one called Nightmare?"

Aw, hell and blast! Could this *get* any worse?

'Don't tell him anything!' I practically screamed into her head.

"It *is,* isn't it?" the Russian was practically *gleeful* at this point!

"Mr. Foyle, you need to come with us!" Earl commanded, reaching for his arm.

"What? Why?" Tim spluttered.

"Because they plan to kill you," Emily informed him, also reaching for the man.

"Nyet!" the Russian sneered. "We would not kill him… right away… He might be useful hostage. Maybe Nightmare would deal for his safety!"

Earl and Emily ignored the man and hauled Tim outside, flinching as bullets struck the doorframe. It was at this point that Emily flung her cup of coffee away from her in favor of using her free hand to reach for the car door handle so that she could forcefully shove Tim into the backseat as Earl raced to start the car, which he slammed into gear before the doors were shut.

"What are we going to do now?" Emily asked, working hard to keep the panic out of her voice.

"We're going to a safehouse," Earl promised.

This sparked an idea that I shared with Emily, the better to keep my cover with Tim.

'Suggest calling the sheriff as backup,' I sent to her. *'Tell Earl that your friend says you can trust her.'*

"Remember my friend?" Emily asked Earl, going along. "The one this loser accused? She's told me before that the sheriff is a trustworthy person."

Before Earl could say anything, I sent a quick, *'Go along with it!'* into his head via the king of hearts card, earning me a huff of emotion telling me he had already *planned* to.

"Yeah?" Earl asked, sounding intrigued. "You think she's a good judge of character?" he added, seeing where we were going.

"Yes!" Tim proclaimed from the backseat. "She's *really* good at reading people! I saw her playing cards and she called *everyone's* bluff!"

"She's been useful to me before," Emily added with a small smirk.

"Like that time in New Orleans?" Earl asked, inwardly gloating at deflating all of Tim's theories about me.

'Tell him I introduced you to my friend, the mambo!' I suggested into her head.

"She's the one that introduced me to the mambo," Emily shrugged. "Broke the case, didn't it?"

"So it did!" Earl agreed. "Alright, then, call the sheriff. We could use some more backup."

I gave Emily the sheriff's number and told her to introduce herself as Agent Dreamer.

"Sheriff Carter?" Emily asked on the phone. "This is Agent Dreamer of the FBI. My friend, *Jane*, told me I could rely on your help."

"Who are you really?" Carter demanded, sounding angry, probably thinking this was some kind of ruse, since the sheriff knew that Dreamer was my alias.

"We're taking one Tim Foyle into protective custody and are fleeing Russian Agents that have infiltrated your town," Emily continued. "We could use some backup, if you're willing. I'll send you the details once I have them."

Emily disconnected somewhat abruptly and I was guessing the sheriff would be *fuming,* so I hastily dialed her phone.

"*What?*" the sheriff demanded angrily.

"Um, hi, sheriff!" I mewled meekly into the phone.

"Jane?" she asked, her tone going to one of astonishment.

"Hey, sorry about that," I apologized pathetically. "Tim's article attracted some unsavory characters so my housemate had to take on the role of Agent Dreamer, but now they're on the run…" I told her in a quick rush.

"You mean that was *real?*" she demanded.

"Afraid so…" I sighed, on the verge of panicking. "Earl and Emily are taking them to a safehouse, but I don't know where, just yet. I think they're kind of winging it, but we could use some more people on our side… So, are you willing to help?"

"Of course!" she scoffed, as if this was a no-brainer.

"Oh, good…" I sighed in relief. "I'm sure Emily or Earl will call with the details."

"I'll be ready," she promised.

I tapped into Earl's mind using the card in front of me, anxious to find out what was to become of me.

'*I'm back,*' I informed him. '*What do you want me to do?*'

"Get with the sheriff," he told me in a quiet whisper low enough that it was likely nobody else heard him. "Have her give you a ride to the store so she can watch over you in the SCIF room. Whatever happens, *you* are the priority here."

'*What about Sarah?*' I asked. '*She came here after she saw Tim's article.*'

Earl swore briefly under his breath before answering, "Alright, I'll clear her for the SCIF room, but *only* if you lock down the computers."

'*Okay,*' I assented, not knowing what else to do.

I let Emily know the plan and suggested that she act like the sheriff would be keeping watch over *them,* instead of *me.* Emily nodded understanding and I trusted her to do her part while I called the sheriff back.

"Jane?" the sheriff greeted as she answered her phone. "What's going on?"

"Earl wants you to give me and Sarah a ride to the store," I answered. After that, he wants you to keep an eye on us to make sure the Russians don't come after us.

"I'll be right there," she assured me.

"Um…" I hesitated as I thought of something. "We don't want to draw attention to ourselves, so…"

"You want me to come in my civilian clothes and car," she finished for me.

"Right," I sighed, glad she understood and hadn't made things awkward.

"It'll take me about twenty minutes to swap out," she informed me. "Will you be all right until then?"

"The kids will keep me safe," I assured her, somewhat grateful for the time it would give me to explain things to Sarah and the kids.

"What's going on?" Sarah asked, sounding anxious.

"You remember the worst-case scenario you envisioned?" I asked. "Well, it's here… Tim's article attracted Prizrak, the Russian version of Aesop and now they're here and they think that Emily, as Dreamer, has ties to the one they call Nightmare, which is to say, *me*."

She let out a shuddering sigh, her face going from fearful to the first shades of terror.

"Earl and Emily are taking Tim to a safehouse," I continued. "They're keeping up the charade I'm just somebody Dreamer barely knows. In the meantime, the sheriff will be driving us to the store and down into the bunker to keep me safe."

"What happens if this doesn't work?" she asked, quietly, fearful of the answer.

"That depends," I answered, solemnly. "Best case? I get out alive and have to move. Worst case, I die…"

"No!" the kids wailed in unison, flying around the room in agitation. "You can't *leave* us!"

"I don't *want* to leave you!" I shouted to them, trying, and failing, to calm them down. "We're just in a serious situation here," I continued, taking a deep breath in an effort to calm myself. "We have to consider the different possibilities. We're going to do everything we can to make sure the worst *doesn't* happen, but we can't blind ourselves to reality."

"Please don't leave us!" Wendy wailed from in front of me.

"We'll keep you safe!" Peter promised.

"I know you would," I cooed to them, stroking their cheeks, their skin feeling ice-cold. "But what if they came here and set fire to the house in order to convince Dreamer to take them seriously?" I asked. "Then, if we ran, they could shoot us down, but if we stayed, we'd be burned alive. And, without the house, what would happen to the two of you?"

Peter and Wendy looked solemn, on the verge of tears.

"Promise you won't die!" Wendy demanded.

"Or, if you do, that you'll come play with us!" Peter added.

"I'll do my best not to die," I promised, avoiding the possibility of coming back as a ghost to haunt this house.

It would be a little while longer before the sheriff came to pick us up, so I checked in with Emily. Earl was driving up to a no-tell motel just outside of town. The motel was kind of stranded in the middle of nowhere, in-between a chain of outlet stores and the town proper. To call it ramshackle would be doing it a *great* favor. Earl pulled into the parking lot and got out, with Emily dragging a protesting Tim behind her.

"Either you shut your mouth," she warned in a deadly cold voice, "or I will feed you your *socks!*" Emily pushed feelings of fear and intimidation towards Tim for emphasis and he cowed under her grip, following where she led.

I confess I was kind of jealous of her just then...

Rather than go in the front way, Earl took a detour around the back of the building and towards a large utility station. The station looked to be one of the bigger ones that kind of looks like a reinforced locker for an extra-large uniform. There were warnings of high voltage plastered on the front to add to the intimidation factor. Earl took a quick glance around to check that nobody was watching them before unlocking the door to reveal a steel ladder set into a concrete tube leading down to some kind of bunker.

Earl took the lead, carefully climbing down the rungs, before calling for Emily, aka Dreamer, to send Tim down. A glare from Emily was enough to convince him that it would be better if he cooperated. Once he was safely down,

Emily took her turn, closing the little door and latching it shut behind her.

Earl's safehouse looked to be an old bunker of some kind. The walls, ceiling, and floor, were all concrete with only a few bulbs illuminating the dingy space. I saw a showerhead set into the ceiling over a metal drain set into the floor, with only a steel rod fastened into the wall, forming a U shape, to serve as a shower-rod bereft of a shower curtain. I also saw something that looked like a combination toilet/sink made out of steel and fastened to a far wall, with zero amenities for privacy. Along another wall, I saw a few cheap army cots that had seen better days. I could barely make out, in the gloom, a set of steel shelves that *might* have held provisions, like food and a first-aid, but it was hard to tell.

I tapped into Earl's mind to get an impression of what the place actually was. His thoughts were centered on the relief he felt that the electricity was still working in the old fallout shelter. From what I could gleam of his thoughts, the bunker had belonged to a private citizen and was built during the Cuban missile scare. The man had died without any family, so his property, including the bunker, had gone to the government. The CIA had acquired it as one of the many heavily fortified, yet hidden, safehouses they had scattered around the country. When Earl had the SCIF room installed, he learned of this bunker and had a phony utility cover built over the door to the bunker to use should he ever need to squirrel me away before moving me somewhere else.

It was a sobering thought, to learn that Earl had prepared for the day I would be discovered and have to move for my own safety. It was downright depressing to think that day could be *here!*

"Just who the hell *are* you people?" Tim wailed.

"It's classified," Earl intoned menacingly.

Tim took a look at his situation, must have realized that he was in a hidden bunker in the middle of nowhere and the only people that knew where he was were the two people who had kidnapped him.

He whimpered pathetically.

I confess that there was a time when I might have *enjoyed* seeing Tim in such a state. Today was not that day, though, seeing as how I was about to find myself in a similar fate.

Aw, hell and blast! Why me?

Chapter 16

Secret War

"You can't keep me here!" Tim whined.

"Watch me!" Earl dared.

"Can you at least tell me what the hell is going on here?" Tim demanded.

Earl sighed and explained, "You dived right into the middle of a war that's been going on since the seventies."

"*What* war?" Tim shrieked.

"The *secret* war, dumbass!" Earl snarled. "Back in the seventies, the powers of the world learned that psychics were *real*. Some psychics are better than others, but some are out-and-out con-men. Every major power in the world has their own version of Aesop, in that they recruit psychics to spy on other governments."

"People like *her?*" Tim demanded, pointing an accusing finger towards Emily, still disguised as Dreamer.

"Exactly," Earl conceded. "Agent Dreamer, here, has the ability to manipulate the emotions of others."

"The others mentioned someone named Nightmare?" Tim asked, looking slightly more comfortable than I would have liked, given the circumstances. I think he had reverted to his journalist mode and investigating what he must have seen as the story of the century.

"Nightmare is our ace in the hole," Earl explained, a menacing tone in his voice. "They have the ability to spy on anyone, anywhere, using just the smallest of focal items. Maybe a knickknack that can be replaced with a replica, or maybe a drop of blood obtained from a medical checkup. They are untraceable, unstoppable, and *perfectly* accurate."

"And *you* just compromised them!" Emily growled viciously.

"What? How was I supposed to know?" Tim quavered.

"By getting your facts straight *before* making wild accusations!" Earl huffed, angrily.

"Then, is *Jane* nightmare?" Tim asked, making my heart stop.

"Jane?" Earl asked, looking confused, playing his part *perfectly*.

"The girl I told you about," Emily threw in, catching the drift. "The one *this* idiot accused. You sent me to New Orleans with her."

"Oh," Earl snorted. "*Her*. No, we looked into her because she seems like she can read minds, but it turns out she's just good at reading people's faces; probably because of her background. She might make a good agent if she didn't have that medical condition."

"Medical condition?" Tim asked, looking genuinely confused.

"Anemia," Emily supplied. "She tends to get winded just walking down the street. Haven't you ever noticed? I mean, she's got the medic-alert bracelet, so it's pretty obvious."

"I thought she was just out of shape…" Tim demurred.

Out of shape? Oh, that miserable *bastard!* I'd slap him upside the head the next chance I got! I could claim I was slapping a mosquito! Yeah! That'd show him!

Some of my irritation *might* have come through my link with Emily because she had to hide some giggles under the guise of coughing…

Oops!

"At most, she's a low-level spooky," Earl threw in. "Not much good to us, so we never pursued her, though Dreamer finds her useful from time-to-time."

"Spooky?" Tim echoed in question.

"Sensitive to ghosts," Emily explained. "It's how she's able to live in a haunted house."

"Wait, ghosts are *real?* " Tim gasped.

Of all the… *gah!* So, Tim thinks that *aliens* and *big foot* and freaking mind-control computer chips are real, but somehow *ghosts* are too far for him?

"Of *course* they're real!" Earl snapped, obviously irritated. "They're just not *reliable!* "

"Ghosts follow their own rules," Emily explained calmly, like she was an expert. "They're limited to where they can go and they're about as reliable as regular people, meaning they can lie to suit their own purposes."

"So…" Tim mumbled, thinking aloud, "then Jane has… *nothing* to do with this?"

"Nothing whatsoever," Earl warned.

"You accused an innocent girl of *treason,*" Emily growled menacingly. "One who has *helped* me several times now."

"*How* has she helped you?" Tim huffed, clearly not believing her.

"Jane has a different background," Emily sighed. "To say that she had a crappy childhood would be an *understatement,* but she somehow survived by learning skills such as being able to read people at a glance, quick memorization, and a naïve mind that doesn't immediately disregard what others would dismiss as impossible."

"But she's always seemed to avoid me…" Tim whined.

"She probably had you pegged inside of five minutes," Earl snorted mercilessly.

"The *last* thing Jane wants is attention," Emily sighed, somewhat soothingly. "Given your actions, that's the *first* thing you want. Is it any *wonder* that she avoids you?"

"Well, when you put it that way…" Tim lamented.

I confess I was getting a little creeped out at how well Earl and Emily seemed to be describing me…

"But what about all those times that Jane was out of town and got hurt?" Tim countered in a last-ditch effort to make his case.

"Isn't it funny how the most fragile people are also the klutziest?" Emily commented with a snort.

"But she was in places where major events happened!" Tim refuted.

"Coincidence," Earl shrugged. "Or it was because Dreamer brought her," he added. "New Orleans was Dreamer's way of assessing her, only she found herself embroiled in the Locked-Room Killer case."

"Jane was supposedly on assignment to find some new exotic merchandise for that little antique store," Emily supplied. "In the course of that, she befriended a mambo who had some… *unorthodox* views on the case, which Jane passed on to me. Anyone else might have dismissed it as insane, but not her. Like I said, she's good at reading people and what she saw in the mambo was honest sincerity."

"Turns out the killer thought the same way as the mambo," Earl continued for Emily, who was guessing at most of the particulars. "Once Dreamer realized that, she laid a trap for him."

"Different perspectives," Emily reiterated. "You'd *know* that if you had taken the time to talk to her, rather than making wild assumptions."

"So, what's going to happen to me?" he asked after a long, awkward silence.

"What's going to happen is this," Earl explained in a matter-of-fact voice. "One, you're never going to speak a *word* of this to *anyone.*"

"Not even Jane," Emily intoned, earning a nod from Earl.

"Two," Earl continued, "you're going to help me whenever, and wherever, I ask for it, because if you *don't,* I put you away for treason down a deep dark hole where *nobody* will ever find you."

"You can't *do* this to me!" Tim protested. "I'm an American citizen!"

"An American citizen that has just *compromised* our most *valuable* asset!" Earl corrected. "Make no mistake, *dumbass*, if it comes to *their* life or *yours,* you can count on me picking *their* life every single time."

There was an audible gulp from Tim. Hell and blast! I never realized Earl could be so menacing!

"And to make sure you behave," Earl continued as he pulled out a blank card and a small pen knife, "you're going to *donate* some of your blood so that Nightmare can keep a *special* eye on you."

At this point, Earl flicked open his pen knife, grabbed Tim's hand, and jabbed the point of the knife into one of Tim's fingers, drawing a large bead of blood. He massaged a few drops of the blood onto the white card until he was satisfied he had enough before releasing Tim's hand. Earl held the card for a few moments, waiting for the blood on it to dry while trying to look nonchalant about it, and failing rather badly.

"What about Jane?" Tim whined pathetically. "What's going to happen to her?"

Funny how he waited so long to consider what might happen to his *victim*, isn't it?

"You mean now that you put a *target* on her back?" Emily snapped.

"I texted the sheriff," Earl interrupted the argument that was sure to ensue from that remark. "She's going to be keeping watch on the girl. I got the impression that the two of them are friends."

"Yeah…" Tim agreed with a sigh. "Ever since Jane found that girl and the sheriff apologized for arresting her, they seem to get along…"

Emily just snorted at this remark, probably to hide the shock I could feel coming from her.

"Jane, the sheriff is here!" Wendy called to me from far away.

'Gotta drop out for a while,' I sent to Emily. *'The sheriff is taking me to the bunker.'*

'I kinda forgot you might still be there…' Emily thought back.

I sent her a small chuckle before disconnecting.

Today had been a rollercoaster of a day, but the day wasn't over yet…

Not by a long shot…

Chapter 17

Strategic Withdrawal

"The sheriff is here to take us to the bunker," I announced to Sarah, still sitting across from me, her face looking a bit worried and ever so slightly impatient.

"How do you know that and what's the bunker?" she asked, her voice broadcasting her anxiety more than her face did.

"Wendy told me the sheriff is here," I sighed as I gathered up my things, like the keychain, the cards, my keys, wallet, and phone. For good measure, I grabbed Mr. Fluffybutt from the seat next to me and placed him in a large shoulder bag. "As for the bunker, it's a SCIF room. Earl had it built for me in the basement of the antique store."

"Oh," she squeaked, a little surprised, but less surprised than I *thought* she'd be, given the circumstances.

"We should meet her outside," I announced, getting up and making my way to the front door. "It's possible the Russians will check out this house before long, if they haven't already."

"Why would they do that?" she asked, a little perplexed, but following me nonetheless.

"One of them is the brother of one that 'disappeared' after coming here before," I explained. "He was looking for my live-in nurse, at the time, but she had moved out by the time he showed up."

"When you say disappeared..." she prompted.

"As in, it's classified," I sighed, fumbling with the doorknob. "Look, he was a bad man and now he won't be hurting anyone else. If it makes you feel any better, he's not dead."

I confess I *might* have muttered, "but he might *wish* he was dead," under my breath, but I'm pretty sure Sarah didn't hear that...

Sheriff Carter, wearing a red tank-top tucked into black jeans, waved to us as we stepped out and we made our way to her civilian SUV that didn't look much different than her departmental SUV. Sarah took the back seat, but the sheriff opened the front passenger door indicating I should sit there. I'm guessing she wanted to talk on our way there… *super…*

"So…" Carter sighed as we got underway, "Russian agents?"

"With Prizrak," I confirmed.

"Prizrak?" she asked, looking like she suspected but still wanted confirmation.

"Russian version of Aesop," I explained. "One of them is a sensitive and the brother of the one that tried to attack me several years ago."

"The one I got a call about a shooting?" she asked for clarification.

"The same," I nodded. "They called him the Black Scorpion and he had the ability to inflict massive amounts of pain with just a touch. His brother is here, probably looking for revenge, and can tell when Emily is manipulating emotions or when I'm talking in her head."

"Jesus!" she whistled.

"It gets better," I continued. "He's teamed up with a big, brutish, hitman that I *know* has already killed at least three women, slitting their throats with a knife or maybe a garotte…"

"Let me guess," she sighed, a little wearily, "more ghosts?"

"Exactly," I confirmed. "They're still in their gory phase, too…" I whimpered slightly.

"Okay, so let me get this straight," she huffed. "The plan is to get you and… I'm sorry, who is this?"

"I'm Sarah!" she declared from the backseat. "Adoptive mother," she added.

The sheriff looked at me, her face clearly asking how much she knew about me.

"She knows more about me than you do, at this point," I answered her unasked question.

"She does?" Carter asked, quirking an eyebrow in disbelief.

"She knows what's in the NDA," I explained.

"I see…" Carter muttered while Sarah just looked smug in the backseat.

She parked across the street from the antique store. It was still pretty bright out, but the street was fairly deserted as all the stores had closed several hours ago. The bright side is that I didn't see anybody watching us, so the store likely wasn't being staked out.

Remember, it's only paranoia if they *aren't* out to get you!

I led everyone around back, unlocking the back door, ushering everyone inside, and locking the door behind me. I, then, unlocked the basement door and shooed everyone down the steps before locking *that* door behind me and inch-worming my way down the stairs.

"So, this is the bunker!" Sarah proclaimed, admiring the large steel door.

"Yep," I huffed, slightly winded. I swiped my card, entered the random number from my key fob, then placed my thumb on the panel. The door unlocked with a loud click and I opened it, motioning for everyone to get inside the airlock chamber. They griped a little at having to give up their phones, but it's not like they would have worked inside the main chamber, anyway.

"Wait here a moment while I secure the computers in the next room," I commanded gently. I got resigned affirmations, which was good enough, so I put my eye up to the scanner, unlocking the inner door.

I rushed to the computers, made sure they were locked down, then reopened the inner door, showing them inside.

"What now?" Carter asked, looking around and seeing only two seats, one in front of the computers and one at a table in front of a video camera on a tripod.

"I'll check in with Earl," I declared, sitting with a small sigh of relief at the folding chair in front of the small table.

I dug out the pack of cards and placed my thumb on the king of hearts, which was still right at the top of the deck.

'Ring-ring!' I sent into his head, announcing myself. Earl was sitting on one of the cots in his own bunker while his mind ran through different scenarios of what might happen and how he should respond to them.

"I hear you," he whispered.

'Sarah, the sheriff, and I are all in the bunker,' I told him. *'What's the plan, now?'* I asked after a moment, when he didn't take the hint.

"Now we wait," he sighed.

'For how long?' I asked.

"Until they make their move or until tomorrow morning," he answered, his voice taking on an edge of determination.

'What about your other agents?' I sent, trying to figure out just how much backup we really had, while also ignoring the possibility of either staying up all night or trying to sleep in a place that really wasn't designed to be slept in.

"Budget cuts," he moaned softly. "Closest agents are hours away and I can't even get them *moving* until tomorrow morning!"

'Did you want the sheriff over there?' I asked. *'I mean, the bunker here isn't really designed to be slept in…'*

"An oversight on my part…" Earl muttered. I could feel him trying to decide which place the Russians were most likely to show up at. Had the Russians followed them out of town, or had they decided to stake out places they knew about? He was picturing the somewhat flimsy lock on the false utility box and how screwed they'd be if they were taken by surprise there. One little grenade would wipe them out! He was also figuring the security cameras in the store would provide the eyes and ears I would need without compromising my position.

"Send the sheriff here," he finally whispered. "You saw where we are, right?"

'I saw,' I affirmed. *'False utility box leading to an underground bomb shelter.'*

"That's the place," he agreed. "Tell her I want her to stake the place out, keep an eye peeled for our targets."

'Will do,' I promised. *'I'll also contact Emily and let her know the plan. It'll keep you from exposing too much to Tim.'*

"Good call," he agreed.

I disconnected and faced the sheriff, who stood over me with her arms crossed. Sarah, meanwhile, was in one of the office chairs in front of one of the computers. They looked like they *might* have had some sort of contest to decide who got to sit and who had to stand. Carter did *not* look pleased to have lost…

"Earl wants you to do a stakeout at their position," I explained to her. "They're just outside of town, at that no-tell motel. Behind the motel is a utility box that's not *really* a utility box. It leads to an underground bunker that used to be a bomb shelter. Earl figures that with the cameras here, I can provide my own stakeout. He also says that we'll likely have to stay in place overnight or until something happens."

"You gonna be okay here?" she asked, somewhat perfunctorily.

"It won't be my first time spending the night here," I commented around a yawn.

"Call me if you need me," she nodded before heading out.

Sarah looked like she was going to say something but I held up a hand and explained hastily, "I need to let Emily know what's going on."

Sarah nodded understanding, though she still looked concerned.

I picked up the keychain and connected to Emily's mind.

Her thoughts were all along the lines of hoping she wouldn't have to spend the night in the stupid bunker.

Well! This should go *splendidly*...

'Ring-Ring!' I sent into her head by way of greeting.

'Jane?' she asked before she caught herself. *'Right, who else would it be?'*

'So, um...' I hedged, knowing this was about to go badly. *'Earl says you'll have to spend the night there...'*

'WHAT?' she *screamed* into my head, her face turning to one of utter fury. I could see Earl chuckling to himself as he must have guessed what was happening.

'Blame Earl, not me!' I demanded. *'The sheriff is on her way to you to make sure nobody tries to get into your bunker. Meanwhile, I'm stuck in the SCIF.'*

'I hate this...' she sent, her irritability coming through clearly. *'And why do you get the cushy job?'* she whined.

'How do I have the cushy job?' I demanded.

'You don't have to keep up a persona with Tim leering at you,' she scoffed angrily.

'Well at least you get a nice cot!' I shot back. *'I'm stuck with a folding chair and a table! Do you know how stiff and sore I'm going to be?'*

'Well, have you ever tried to get to sleep on a flimsy cot in a room full of strangers?' she demanded.

'Yes!' I declared vehemently. *'When I was in the sex cult, I had to do exactly that and it was still better than the bed I had growing up!'*

I confess I gave her the mental equivalent of sticking my tongue out at her. Yeah, I'm not proud of that, but she had it coming!

Emily half-groaned, half-sighed in exasperation.

'Hot damn you are competitive!' she asserted after a moment.

'Don't blame me that you've had a pampered life so far!' I refuted.

Emily was now rubbing the bridge of her nose, and I could feel her frustration. She wanted to whine and complain about how bad she had it to garner sympathy, but she could see that it wasn't going to happen with me.

'Look, for what it's worth,' I sighed into her head. *'I envy the fact that you had a childhood and loving parents. My life was all about survival and it's hard for me to not worry about that kind of thing. For me, love, safety, and security were foreign concepts, just words people made up that didn't really mean anything.'*

'Crappy childhood,' she agreed.

I disconnected without remarking as I was already getting tired from using my ability so much. I could sort-of sympathize with her, but at the same time, I felt like she should grow the hell up, which is damned frustrating!

Still, though… she was in this situation because of me… well, me and *Tim,* the weaselly bastard…

"Sorry about that," I apologized to Sarah.

"I understand," she declared agreeably.

"Now, what was it you wanted to say?" I prompted.

"I was just wondering where the beds were…" she answered, looking around the small room.

"Nearest thing to a bed is a sofa outside," I yawned. "You should take that."

"But then, where will *you* sleep?" she demanded, clearly not liking the idea at all.

"Right here," I told her, laying my head in my arms, matching my actions to my words.

"No you're *not!*" she insisted. "You will take the couch and I'll… I'll just stay up all night!"

"But I'm not allowed to leave the bunker, remember?" I chided as gently as I could. "Besides, my ability tends to drain me, so getting to sleep won't be a problem. I'll be stiff and sore tomorrow morning, but that's hardly unusual."

"Then take this," she commanded, taking off a diamond ring from her left hand.

I hesitatingly took it, holding it gently in my fingertips.

"What for?" I asked, not fully understanding, though I suspected why she was doing this.

"I'll sleep on the sofa outside," she explained. "If you need to reach me, or if you see me banging on the door outside, you can use this to get in touch."

I nodded before testing the connection, finding a *strong* connection, like skin-to-skin or blood strong! I delved a little deeper to be sure it connected to *her* and not somebody else, just to be sure.

What I saw through her eyes was a girl that was entirely too thin and worn out trying to play at being an adult because she never learned how to be a child. The girl was staring vacant-eyed at the wedding ring she held in her hands, with tears threatening to overflow while she fought valiantly to keep them from showing. The girl was putting up a façade of being strong when really, she just wanted to hide how powerless she must feel inside.

I fumbled the ring, panicking as it bounced off the table and rolled to the floor!

Sarah, possibly expecting something like this, snatched the ring from the floor before it could slide somewhere out of reach.

"Sorry about that," I mumbled.

"Don't worry about it," she smiled, her look one of loving understanding.

Without another word, she exited the room, leaving me alone in the most secure room in the town, *including* the jail.

It was a long night for everyone else, but for me, it was all too short.

Little did I know that I would need all the sleep I could get for the trials that would come the next morning…

Chapter 18

Hostage

I'm stumbling through a cemetery, going as fast as I can, but hands are grabbing my feet, tripping me as I try to escape the horrors coming after me in the deep dark of a moonless night. I can hear their shuffling, shambling, footsteps mixed in with their moans of agony and despair. I know I *must* get away from them because if I don't, I will surely die and become one of them. I can feel them getting closer, their gurgling cries growing louder, more insistent. Their tone changes, slightly, from one of anger and hatred to one of expectant excitement at the prospect of adding another to their ranks. I scramble on my hands and knees, trying desperately to get away, but they keep coming! Closer… *closer!*

I awoke with a start, my heart beating a fast staccato in my chest as I sit in a hard chair panting in a futile effort to keep up with the demands of my heart.

It takes me a long moment for my mind to get in gear, for the memories to come back to me, and to realize where I am and why…

I'm in the bunker, sitting in an uncomfortable folding chair, sleeping on a hard, wooden, table, because I'm trying to escape the clutches of foreign agents that would love nothing better than to capture me and torture me into revealing all I know to them.

With that realization comes a small relief, because I know I am safe and *not* in a dreaded cemetery.

Yet something feels *off*… Something prickles my sense of peace and well-being… what is it?

I confess it takes me longer than I would like, to realize what's wrong. The gurgling cries I heard in the nightmare linger; I can still hear them!

Wait… why can I still hear them? Think, Jane, *think!*

The hitman! It *must* be him! And he must be close! Aw, hell and blast! Has he already found me?

I pick up Sarah's wedding ring and peak into her head. She's dreaming of wandering, lost, through a building that is both familiar and, yet, strangely alien. She doesn't hear the wet, gurgling, cries of revenge that I do.

'Sarah... Sarah!' I send into her head, trying to be gentle, while also needing her to wake up. I can feel her stirring while her mind incorporates me into her dream, now showing me near her, while the path to me is obstructed. Sometimes it's a glass window, sometimes it's a partition, but the path to me is never straightforward and every route she takes seems to bring her no closer to me.

'Sarah, wake up!' I shout into her head, jerking her awake with a start.

"Wha?" she mumbles, groggily, her head still foggy from sleep.

'Sarah, I'm opening the doors. You need to get into the bunker, now!' I command as I hastily get up and desperately fumble open the inner door, hopping on one leg to the outer door and flinging it open, leaning on it for support as I wave Sarah inside.

"What's going on?" she asked, her voice taking on an edge of panic.

I slam the outer door shut, locking it automatically, and shoo her through the airlock and into the bunker proper.

I don't answer her until we're both inside and the door has been locked tight.

"I think the hitman is close by," I pant, hopping back to the chair I had slept in and desperately hoping I didn't fall because, with my luck, I'd break something *else!*

"Did you see him on the monitors?" she asked, glancing over at the screens showing the feed from the security cameras.

I might have blushed because I didn't even *think* of those, while I was panicking, as I desperately worked to make sure Sarah had gotten safely back inside.

"The hitman has several ghosts anchored to him," I explained, somewhat hastily while I tried to think through what I should do next. "I can hear *them,* so he must be close by!

Sarah whirled on me, perhaps realizing, for the first time, what my ability to see ghosts meant for me. I guess knowing that I can see ghosts, as an abstraction, and seeing the kids show-off at the house is one thing, but understanding that I can see the ghosts of victims anchored to their killer and instantly know, beyond a shadow of a doubt, that I was facing someone that could, and *would,* kill me without a moment's hesitation is an *entirely* different matter.

"I gotta tell Earl that they're here…" I muttered, more to myself than to her.

Earl would know what to do, surely!

I place my fingers on the king of hearts and enter Earl's head. He's already awake and considering his course of action.

'Ring-fucking-ring!' I practically shout into his head.

"Jane? What's wrong?" he whispers, startled.

'I think the hitman is here!' I proclaim.

"Do you see him on the monitors?" he asked.

I hastily glance over at the monitors, checking both the cameras outside as well as those within the store, but don't see anyone.

'He's not on the monitors, but I can hear the ghosts anchored to him!' I tell him urgently.

"We're on our way," he tells me as he gets up. "Whatever happens, do *not* leave the bunker!"

I disconnect without promising *anything,* because, just then, I saw Anne on the monitors showing the back door. She's coming in to open the store for the day, but right behind her is a large man holding a gun! Before she can lock the door, he shoves the gun in her terrified face and shoves her into the store!

Coming in behind the large man with the gun is the sensitive that scares me more than the hitman. I can see him giving orders, but I can't hear him. Anne tries to run, probably hoping she can get out the front door and scream for help, or something, but the larger man grabs her hair and yanks her back! I can see tears in her eyes as she starts whimpering, probably begging for her life!

"Jane, you need to stay *here!"* Sarah insists, reading my face and seeing that I'm about to charge headlong into danger.

"But they'll *kill* her!" I grind out.

"They'll keep her alive," she asserts. "They *need* her alive because they hope to use *her* to get to *you!"*

"But they don't *know* that I'm Nightmare!" I almost shout.

"But they know you're connected to Dreamer and Dreamer knows Nightmare," Sarah explains, her voice going cold with the logic of it all.

I knew Sarah was right, *damn* it all! Sarah was thinking more clearly than I was at this point because fear was overwhelming me. I don't make friends easily or quickly. I cultivate my friends with the utmost care, choosing who I get close to and getting to know them as well as I can before opening up to them. I choose quality over quantity and I can count the number of people I consider my friends on *one hand!*

So, when one of those friends is being threatened, I *lose my shit* over it, okay?

But fear and panicking wouldn't save her, would it? I *had* to save her. Period. End of discussion. That just wasn't up for debate!

The question is *how?*

I needed to take a mental step back, see the whole picture, not just part of it. I acknowledged my fear for what it was: motivation. I accepted my fear as a warning alarm spurring me to action, but I would not let it control me.

I ran through the exercise Dr. Theodore Bear, my psychiatrist, taught me. I mentally reviewed the entire inventory of the antique store, mentally walking through it and naming the items, one-by-one. When I had done that in English, and still felt fear threatening to overwhelm me, I did it in German, then Russian, and finally Korean.

Doing this cost me a whopping five minutes and I saw Anne pulling out her phone, making a call, likely to my phone which was tucked away in the airlock, a room without reception. Her face was one of terror as a gun was held just inches away from her eyes.

Earl was on his way, but he was still likely fifteen to twenty minutes out. Anne could be *dead* by then.

If I was going to save her, I'd need to do it *soon*.

Okay, what advantages did I have? Well, I had the security monitors, showing me where they were within the store. I had more information than they did about what was *really* going on.

And I was an expert on ghosts…

The idea crystallized within my head and an utterly *insane* plan sprang forth, quickly building up details as I thought it through.

Ghosts become stronger with belief. Ghosts can hear me even when I barely whisper to them. People who are not normally sensitive to ghosts can become sensitized to them with just a little belief, which, in turn, makes ghosts that much stronger!

Was it dangerous? Oh, you *bet!*

Would it work? Probably not.

Did I have any *other* ideas? *Nope!*

Was I going to do it? You damned well better believe it!

But I would need help…

I picked up Emily's keychain and connected to her mind. She was groggy and bitter at having to sleep on a musty old cot.

'Emily, I need your help!' I almost shout into her head, startling her.

'What do you want now?' she griped.

'Anne has been taken hostage,' I tell her, trying to impart the seriousness of the situation.

'Dammit,' she sent back, but with less grief or sorrow as I would have liked.

'Listen, I've got a plan, but I need your help,' I insist.

'The only plan you need is to stay put!' she snarled.

'But if I do that, she'll die!' I shot back, angrily.

'It happens,' she stated flatly.

'Not to me, it doesn't!' I growled.

Emily actually *chuckled* at this! The sheer *audacity!*

'It is not funny!' I huffed, rage filling me.

'Look, Jane, you need to understand something,' she asserted, feeling superior to me. *'Right now, you are more valuable than she is! If they've taken Anne hostage, it's to get to you! Understand?'*

'Do you understand that if I don't do anything, she will die?!' I screamed into her head, making her wince.

'And if you get killed,' she countered, *'then America is worse off than if she dies. You have a duty to keep yourself safe, even if it means sacrificing another. I thought you, of all people, would understand that the world is a harsh place and the business we are in is life-and-death. If Anne dies, but you*

don't, then it's an acceptable loss. If you can't accept that, then you need to grow up!'

    'Anne is not an acceptable loss!' I whined. *'Not to me!'*

    'We all lose friends,' Emily lamented, somewhat bitterly.

    'Listen here!' I gruffed, tears coming to my eyes. *'I've got a plan that I'm doing, with or without your help! My plan has a helluva lot better chance at succeeding if you help me! Now, will you help me?'*

    'Fine…' Emily relented. *'What do you want me to do?'*

    'When you get here, look the tall one in the eyes and tell him that hitmen are often haunted by their victims,' I tell her, briefly outlining part of my plan to her. *'Maybe ramp up the fear while you're doing it. And, if you can, try to work the way he kills his victims into whatever dialogue you have with him.'*

    'What are you planning to do?' she asked, feeling nervous.

    'The enemy of my enemy…' I answered cryptically, fearing that if I told her too much, she might chicken out, which would seriously hamper my plan.

    'Dammit, you're planning to use ghosts, aren't you?' she sighed, rubbing the bridge of her nose.

    'Don't worry,' I soothed. *'They won't be after you.'*

    'You know Earl is going to kill you for this, right?' she chuckled.

    'Pfft!' I scoffed. *'At this point, I don't care. So, will you do it?'*

    'Alright, fine! I'll do it!' she relented. *'I'll even keep it from Earl, okay?'*

    'Perfect!' I agreed before disconnecting.

    I sat at the table panting, cursing how worn-out I now felt after such a long conversation. The urge to take a nap was strong, but I had more work to do. I had to think ahead as far as I could. If my plan went sideways, as I figured it almost certainly *would,* I had to be prepared for the worst to happen.

    I took off my pendant from around my neck. It was a gift and meant a lot to me, so it had deep emotional ties. Deep emotional ties meant it could be used against me by another sensitive. Same with my medic-alert bracelet, so it had to go too. I laid both items on the table next to Sarah's ring, the pack of cards, and the keychain.

I picked up the ring and offered it back to Sarah, who was giving me a stern look, like she knew I was planning something that was likely to get me killed, captured, or *worse*.

Guess that comes from being a mother…

"What are you planning to do?" she demanded, her voice one of caution, neither stern, nor gentle. It was the voice of a parent that knows their child has been misbehaving but doesn't want *them* to know that they know.

"I'm going to save Anne," I declared. "I need you to keep these safe," I told her, gesturing to the items on the table.

"You are *not* going out there!" she insisted, blocking my way.

"I *am* going out there!" I growled. *"Nobody* gets to decide whose life has value and whose life *doesn't!* Not *you,* not *Earl,* not *Emily!"*

"And what about *you?"* she retorted. "Doesn't *your* life have value?"

"No more value than Anne's life," I stated calmly. "My life is my own. Shouldn't *I* be the one to decide what to do with it?"

"Your life is *not* your own!" she declared, vehemently. "It hasn't been your own for a long time, now! Your life is *shared* with those who love you! Don't *we* get a say in it?"

"You've *had* your say," I told her, tears threatening my eyes even as my resolve deepened. "You've been overruled. It's *my* life, so *I* have the final say in it. My plan *can* work! I *refuse* to lose *anybody else!* I lost Tommy through carelessness; I lost Sha-De through circumstance, and I'll be *damned* if I'm going to lose Anne when I have the power to *save* her! Now, either move out of my way, or I'll *make* you move!"

"And just how are you going to do that?" she asked, sounding more curious than angry.

In answer I held up my hand and stated, "I've hurt people before, using my ability. I've manipulated them, too! Do you *really* want to see how far I'll go?"

Sarah must have seen the conviction in my eyes as she finally relented, sighing heavily as she sank into the office chair in front of the monitors.

Part of my mind cautioned me that I had just hurt one of the few people I care about. Another part of my mind told me my relationship with her could be repaired, but if Anne died, there was no getting her back.

I chose forgiveness over permission.

Focus, Jane. Work the problem at hand. Do what it takes to survive.

Earl would be here in ten minutes, give or take. That's how long I had to get my plan up and running.

I moved into the airlock, taking my phone from its lockbox. The room had no reception. I'd have to wait until I was in the basement to see the message Anne likely left for me. I briefly considered leaving my phone in the airlock, since it, too, was an emotional connection to me, but ultimately decided to take it with me on the grounds that it would be more useful to me, as a phone, than to another psychic as a focal object.

I left the bunker and was in the basement of the store when my phone alerted me to a new voicemail. I typed in my passcode and held the phone to my ear, hoping nobody upstairs would hear it.

"Jane? It's Anne…" came the message. I could hear a quaver in Anne's voice. Even if I *hadn't* seen Anne being held hostage, I would have known something was wrong from the fear I heard in her voice. "I need you to come in earlier than usual… I've got some… uh… new merchandise I want you to look over!"

"I'm coming for you, Anne…" I whispered my promise to the empty room.

Chapter 19

Showdown

Okay, so first things first... I needed to get upstairs without anyone hearing me come up from the basement, then convince them that I had come in from outside. I realized, belatedly, that I could have *really* used the security monitors in the other room. If I had held onto Sarah's ring, I could have used her eyes to watch the monitors and see where everyone was before making my way into the store proper.

Oh well, it would have also meant risking that damned sensitive sensing what was happening and ambushing me. Given how crazy my plan was, to begin with, any unnecessary risk should be avoided, if at all possible.

I inch-wormed my way up the stairs one step at a time and waited at the top step, pressing my ear to the door, listening for where the activity was while also picturing the layout of the store. Did the back door have any windows? No, it just has the door without so much as a peep hole in the door, which means they'd be keeping an eye on the *front* of the store, without paying any attention to the *back* of the store.

I unlocked the basement door and open it the tiniest sliver, just *barely* enough to see out of, hoping against hope that the hinges don't squeak.

You know, there are a lot of details in the world that you wouldn't realize might come in useful later on, under unique circumstances. Details like whether the hinges of doors squeak or not, for instance! For the *life* of me, I could not remember if they squeaked before or not! Hell and blast! If they squeaked *now,* I'd be *screwed!*

I tried to minimize this small calamity as much as I could by opening the door as slowly as I could. Thankfully, luck seemed to be on my side, at least for the moment. No squeak, creak, or groan!

Whew!

My heart was beating a pace to make a hummingbird worry for its health as I made my way, ever so slowly, into the hall, all my senses on high alert as they expected someone to step out into the hall and ask what the hell I was doing there. Another stroke of luck is that the basement door is right next to the back door, the better to move things around, I guess, so even if I *was* caught, I could claim that I came in from the back, rather than up from the basement.

I opened the back door, again as slowly and as quietly as I could, and hobbled outside, closing the door behind me.

I confess that I entertained some dark thoughts right about here. I could run, so to speak, away from all this. I could leave Anne to her fate. I might have even rationalized it by convincing myself that they *probably* wouldn't have killed her. They *might* have let her go if I never showed up. I could assure my safety if I just… *left!* Earl could deal with the two agents, right? I mean, he'd be there in about five or ten minutes, or so, right? He's got a gun! Have gun, will kill, right?

But, could I *really* live with myself if I did that? Could I just abandon my *friend?* A friend who *trusted* me? One of the few people on the *planet* that I trusted enough with my secrets?

No. No, I could not. Come what may, I couldn't do that to her. I *would* save her, no matter the cost.

At this point, I figured I was close enough to start the next part of my plan, which is to say the *heart* of it. I needed to get the ghosts haunting the hitman as *strong* as I could as *fast* as I could.

"Hear me, oh ghosts haunting their killer," I whispered in Russian as quietly as I could, knowing that they'd be able to hear me. "I can see you; I can hear you; listen to me; heed my call!"

Okay, yes, it was a bit melodramatic, but something like this *should* be melodramatic! Hell and blast, I'm betting I was the first person they'd ever *met* that could see *and* hear them!

The gurgling moans quieted down for a moment, telling me that they had heard me just fine, so I continued.

"I can help you exact your revenge," I continued whispering in Russian. "You are dead now, and the dead follow different rules. Know this: *believing* is *being!* You need not suffer with your throats cut! Believe that you are healthy and whole and you *will* be!"

Please let this work, please let this work!

I held my breath for a long moment, listening as the wet gurgling sounds died down to nothing and then, a sweet voice called out, "It worked! I can talk again! Close your eyes and think about what it was like *before!*"

Yes! Okay, so far, so good! I waited to the count of thirty before unlocking the back door, making no attempt to be quiet any longer, and called out, "Anne! I got your message and came as soon as I could!" as I stepped into the hallway.

"Jane?" came Anne's voice, which was *just* this side of terrified. "Jane, *run! It's a trap!*"

I heart a meaty *thwack* followed by something that wounded like a sack of potatoes hitting the floor.

"Anne?" I called out, acting my part of oblivious store employee. "What's wrong?"

I was halfway down the hall before the two men stepped out from the front, guns pointed at me.

"How did you get in here?" the smaller man asked.

"Through the back… door…" I answered slowly, acting out a fear that wasn't entirely feigned. To add to it, I started slowly backing down the hall.

"Stop!" the leader commanded, his voice one of absolute authority. "If you run, we will *kill* your friend!"

At this, the taller of the two, the hitman, jerked Anne up violently, and held her to his chest, pulling out a knife and holding it to her throat.

"He'll do it! He will! He *enjoys* it!" the three ghosts called out in Russian, now looking *much* better than before. I made a point of looking each of them in the eyes and nodding ever so slightly to them. Interaction would strengthen them and I needed them as strong as they could be.

"Okay!" I cried out, putting a quaver in my voice. "I'll do whatever you want! Just *please* don't hurt her!"

"You did not come down the street," the leader declared. "We were watching for you, but did not see you."

"A-anne's call sounded urgent," I explained, coming up with a lie on the spot. "So, I got here as fast as I could! A friend gave me a lift, but they were going to a store behind us, and they didn't want to go out of their way! They dropped me off around back and I cut behind their store and came in the back way!"

I was panting by this time, working on selling my fear. I confess I *might* have been hamming it up a bit, but the two men didn't seem to notice.

"That cast, is it real?" the leader questioned, walking towards me.

"Yes!" I whimpered. "I fell down some stairs recently and broke my leg!"

"Let's test it!" he suggested maliciously. He kicked one of my crutches out of my hand, sending me toppling to the ground! I screamed half in surprise and half in pain, especially when my foot landed badly and I could feel a slight grinding in my leg.

I screamed long and loud when the little bastard *kicked* my cast, unleashing a flood of red-hot agony in my leg!

"Stop!" Anne demanded from the hit-man's grip. "You're hurting her!"

"And I'll hurt her *worse* if she doesn't cooperate!" the man retorted.

"What do you *want?*" I cried, tears coming easily to my eyes.

"I want you to call your friend," he demanded, squatting down and jerking my chin up to look him in the eyes. "Your FBI friend!"

"What FBI friend?" I shrieked, remembering that I had told him Dreamer was with corporate.

"Dreamer!" he shouted at me angrily.

"But she's not *with* the FBI!" I whined. "She's with *corporate!*"

"She lied to you!" he smirked. "Now *call* her!"

I dug out my phone from my pocket with shaky hands, going as slow as I dared, and whispering, still in Russian, "Tell me your names so that I might know you."

"I am Irina!" came one voice.

"I am Galina!" came another voice.

"I am Khristina!" came the third voice.

"Irina, Galina, and Khristina!" I echoed, dialing in Emily's phone number by hand. "I hear you! I believe in you!"

I could hear the women cheering before my phone connected to Emily's phone.

"Dreamer?" I squeaked into the phone.

I had the phone in my hand just long enough to hear Emily yell out, "Jane? Jane!" before the leader grabbed the phone out of my hand and started making demands.

"Come to antique store!" he commanded into the phone. "Be here in ten minutes or I *kill* your friend!" To emphasize this, if only to me, he pointed the gun at me, still prone on the floor.

"Don't shoot!" I screamed, mostly to play my part, but partly because I worried that he really *would* shoot me, since I was no longer useful and would only serve to slow them down.

Hell and blast! Why didn't I think of that *before?*

I hoped that he would keep me alive at *least* until they got here, which should be any minute now! *Please?*

I resumed my whispering to the ghosts in Russian as quietly as I could. I hoped that if the men overheard me, they would mistake it for prayer or something. I was telling the ghosts the new rules that they lived by, namely that they were anchored to their killer and gained power from belief. I reinforced this by staring at the three women, each lovely after a fashion, and hoping that they would be strong enough to reduce the number of agents we were dealing with down to one.

The smaller man kicked my broken leg again, eliciting another scream from me before demanding, "Get up!"

"I *can't!*" I cried. "My leg is *broken!*"

"I said *get up!*" he demanded again, pointing the gun at my head.

I did my best to push myself up to a sitting position, trying to get my good leg under me, and reaching for a crutch. The man seemed impatient, but he left me to struggle to my foot, leaning on the one crutch I could reach.

"Over to the register!" he commanded, shoving me hard enough that I almost fell again.

I saw an opportunity, here, and reached out a hand to the three ghosts as surreptitiously as I could. I brushed my hand against their arms, startling them and filling their faces with a bit of wonder that they could feel me and I could feel them.

Granted, my hand was numb from the freezing cold that comes from touching a ghost in that way, but it made them stronger, for sure!

"May you be haunted by those you killed!" I snarled at the two men as I sat heavily in the little stool at the register.

Now that the ghosts were stronger, I needed to add to the hitman's belief in order to sensitize him to those he killed.

I just hoped he understood English! It'd be weird for a retail worker in Iowa to know Russian!

My oath earned me a hard slap in the face from the leader, which would bruise heavily before too long.

But it was worth it because the larger man, still holding Anne, jerked at this. I saw his eyes go wide and it looked like he began to wonder if he was hearing things.

"It's working!" I assured the ghosts. "Yell at him! Scream at him! Call out your names! Hell, call out *his* name! He might hear you!"

The ghosts obeyed and things got noisier, at least for me, in the few minutes it took for Earl and Emily, still disguised as Flagg and Dreamer, showed up, their guns drawn. The leader, obviously expecting this, had put his gun to the side of my head, while the other man was off to the side, his knife still at Anne's throat.

I briefly wondered where the sheriff was, but I guessed that she might be babysitting Tim at the moment.

"Let them go!" Emily demanded. Her gun was pointing at the hitman while Earl's gun was targeting the leader, who was still holding me hostage.

Please let Earl be a good shot! If he *has* to shoot, please let him be a good shot!

Emily was edging towards the hitman, possibly trying to get into range of her ability, but the man was already looking close to panicking.

"How many women have you killed?" Emily asked the hitman. "I'll bet you've killed at least *three!* I'll bet you *slit their throats!"*

The hitman was edging ever closer to out-and-out panic and I guessed that Emily was pushing him with her mind, but the sensitive either wasn't paying attention to her, since he was too busy arguing with Earl, or maybe the training we had done with her ability was paying off and she was able to focus it to a fine edge.

Either way, the man was getting *spooked!*

Earl and the leader continued shouting at each other, each demanding the other put their gun down while threatening to shoot.

I bit down on my lip to resist the temptation to touch my hostage-taker on the arm or leg or something and maybe try to *coax* his thoughts down another track, like I did back in the cult, but the man was a sensitive and whatever I did, I couldn't let him know I was the *real* prize!

Luckily, I didn't have to fight the temptation long because the hitman *screamed* and threw Anne to the floor before waving his knife around at the three ghosts that were now *laughing* at his terror!

I chose this moment to get the hell out of Earl's way and fell out of the stool, hoping against hope that the agent was too distracted by his comrade freaking the fuck out to notice me in time to shoot me before Earl shot *him!*

I landed heavily on the floor behind the register, just barely breaking my fall enough so as not to further damage my leg, and that's when all hell broke loose.

Shots rang out and I heard the man that had been holding me hostage swear in Russian before beating a hasty retreat, dragging his comrade with him.

"Do we go after them?" Emily asked.

"No," Earl decided. "We got what we needed from them."

Earl came around to the register and stood over me, glaring with a wrath that was *biblical!*

"Um… sorry?" I squeaked, halfheartedly.

Yeah… I wasn't sorry, not even a little.

Chapter 20

Spycraft

"You three," Earl growled, pointing to me, Anne, and Emily, "basement! Now!"

Anne helped me hobble to my feet, handed me a crutch, then fetched the other one. My leg was damned painful, and I vowed to see a doctor as soon as I could, but I had more immediate worries, namely the two Russian agents that had beaten a clean retreat, not to mention the wrath of Earl.

Emily went first, with Anne insisting on going last, in case anything happened to me on the way down. Earl stayed upstairs doing who knows what. I figured I knew what was coming and I was steeling myself against the onslaught that I was sure was coming.

Wearily, I waved to the camera in front of the bunker, motioning for Sarah to come outside. A few seconds later, I heard the muffled clicks and thud of the inner door unlocking, shutting, and relocking. A few seconds after *that,* Sarah came out, looking both anxious and slightly relieved.

"Sarah, meet Anne," I introduced. "Anne, this is Sarah, my foster mother."

"How do you do?" Anne greeted feebly, still clearly shaken up by what she just went through.

"Better than you, I suspect…" Sarah remarked, not unkindly.

Anne turned to me, despair on her face, "I'm so *sorry* I lured you into that trap! They *made* me do it! They held a *gun* on me!"

"I know," I consoled. "I was… down here, in the bunker, there, when they grabbed you…"

"You *knew?"* she gasped, grief turning to rage. "And you came *anyway?"*

"I *had* to!" I cried. "If I didn't, they would have *killed* you!"

"Better *me* than *you!"* she despaired.

"Why does everyone keep *saying* that?" I wailed, *furious* that people were treating someone's *life* as if it was some… some bit of *merchandise* on a shelf or something!

"Because it's true," Emily shot back, bluntly. "No offense, Anne, but if the world lost you, the loss would be fairly minimal."

"Yeah…" Anne agreed. "I can't save *anyone*… not like Jane can…"

"You saved *me!*" I retorted. "I came to you with *zero* life skills, a suspicious name, and almost *no* education to speak of! *Despite* that, you gave me a job and helped me when I needed it. You helped me save that girl and you kept me on when you had no real reason to… So, *stop* saying that *your* life is worth less than *mine!*"

"If I had *my* way," Earl gruffed as he came down the stairs, "you'd be *locked up* for disobeying orders!"

"I had a *plan!*" I insisted. "A plan that *worked!*"

"I'm still unclear on what your plan *was…*" Sarah remarked.

"The hitman had three ghosts anchored to him," I started explaining, then saw Anne's confused face turn to one of horror.

"Sorry, Anne…" I sighed. "I forgot you didn't know that part about me… Ghosts are real and I can see and hear them. My house really *is* haunted by a couple of kids named Peter and Wendy. Talking to ghosts make them stronger, and so does belief in them."

"And…" Anne spluttered, looking like she was facing information overload, "you've known about this for… how long?"

"My whole life," I lamented. "My first friend was a ghost."

"Getting back to your 'plan'…" Earl retorted impatiently.

"The hitman had three ghosts anchored to him," I started explaining again. "My plan was to make them as strong as I could as quickly as I could. If I could get *him* believing in them, then he might become sensitive to them, and if *that* happened, it would remove him from the equation!"

I confess I felt rather proud of my plan, especially given that it had *worked,* more or less, exactly as I had planned!

"Which still left the man with the gun…" Emily remarked, shooting down my elation.

"I'm sorry, but who are you?" Anne asked, looking at Emily.

Emily sighed, taking off her sunglasses and started speaking normally again, in an octave more familiar to her.

"Oh!" Anne gasped.

"Jane, you can *have* Agent Dreamer," Emily snorted, handing me back the fake ID and badge.

"What?" Anne spluttered, clearly confused.

"Agent Dreamer of the FBI is an alias I use…" I sighed, taking the proffered items and tucking them away. "She comes in handy when I need to be places a civilian isn't normally allowed. "Emily had to do it this time because, well…" I glanced down at my leg, still in its cast. The pain had dulled to an annoying throb, which I hoped was a good sign.

At this, Anne collapsed onto the sofa, putting her head in her hands.

"So!" Earl reiterated. "Your 'plan' was to make the hitman freak out, which may, or may *not,* have led to him disabling himself, leaving only the sensitive with the *gun* pointed at your head? Does that about sum it all up?"

"Well, I was kind of… hoping that the hitman would… take out the other man?" I cajoled, hoping Earl would see what a good plan it was, rather than the desperate half-assery it really was.

Earl took several deep breaths, looking like he was trying to control his rage at me before he finally muttered, "The *only* reason you're not *dead* right now is that you got *damned* lucky! There's no *way* your plan should have *worked!"*

"Hey now!" I shot back, angrily. "I hedged my bets as much as I *could* have! I told Emily to mention the hitman's victims *and* got her to ramp up his fear *without* the sensitive noticing!"

"I've been practicing!" Emily purred.

"Good work on that," Earl relented, making it obvious he was talking to Emily and not me.

"It was Jane's idea," she shrugged, giving me a wink.

This took Earl aback for a moment as he reconsidered his position.

"What do you mean it was Jane's idea?" he asked, suspiciously.

"I mean," Emily clarified, "that Jane is the one that suggested a way for me to focus my ability on a single person, which also happens to extend my range!"

"Jane did that?" Earl remarked.

"Yep!" I declared, more than a little proud. "All it took was another perspective!"

"That doesn't change the fact that your plan was half-assed at *best!*" Earl retorted angrily.

"Enough!" Sarah shouted, looking like she was at the end of her rope. "What's done is *done!* What are you going to do *now?"*

"And where's Tim?" I asked, not entirely liking his absence; it made me suspicious.

"The sheriff took him back to his house under guard," Earl muttered, pinching the bridge of his nose.

"And what do we do about the Russian agents?" Emily asked, looking mildly irritated.

"I winged the sensitive back there," Earl remarked. "So we've got blood either from the bullet or from the floor around him. Either way, Jane can track him down and bring him to our side."

"We're not taking him in?" I asked, a little bewildered at this.

"As a spy," Earl explained with a small smile on his face, "when you learn of an enemy spy in your territory, the *dumbest* thing you can do is to arrest them. Once they're off the board, their country will just send in a *new* spy, except you won't know who they are! No, it's better to make him an asset."

"You want him to turn double-agent?" I clarified. "Just how do you expect me to do that?"

"By threatening to do to *him* what you did to his *brother!"* Earl smirked, maliciously.

"What did you do to his brother?" Anne asked, quietly. "No, you know what? I don't wanna know!" she wailed, putting her head back in her hands, like she was trying to fit her world back in the box she had it in before.

Poor Anne...

"So, I tell him to cooperate or else I'll give him nightmares?" I lamented.

"Exactly," Earl agreed. "We'll wait a day, though. We don't want him thinking that Nightmare is too close!"

The impromptu meeting broke up shortly after that. Anne closed the store for the day and Earl brought in a forensic team to collect blood samples. Emily drove me to the hospital and I got x-rays of my leg. The cast had cushioned the kicks, somewhat, so the damage wasn't *too* great, but the doctor warned it had likely set my recovery time back. By then, the bruise on my face had blossomed and a nurse quietly questioned me if there was trouble at home. I made up a lie, telling her that a stranger, *not* a romantic interest, had accidently slapped me in the face when they were reaching for something. I further mollified their concern by telling them that I bruise *really* easily.

The doctor prescribed some mild prescription painkillers, which I probably wouldn't take, and sent me on my way.

At my suggestion, in an effort to try to keep the rumors at bay, Emily tracked down Beth and told her that someone had tried to *rob* the antique store and that it would be closed for the day while they cleaned up. We figured with Beth on the case, the story of a robbery would reach every busybody in town inside of a day or two, and would nicely explain any gunshots anyone heard, not to mention the store closing unexpectedly.

However, it was just my damned luck that the story *I* ended up hearing about it had been embellished to the point where I was some kind of damned *hero!* There was talk about how I had, *single-handedly* mind you, stopped two armed robbers, who got away with *nothing!*

This, particular, story has even ended up in several biographies of me…

Looking back, I was an absolute *idiot* for attempting such a cockamamie plan… especially given that I probably could have accomplished much the same end from the security of the bunker. I mean, if I could hear the ghosts, then they surely could have heard *me,* right?

As much as I am *loathed* to admit it, there is the distinct possibility that Earl, might have been, *maybe,* a little bit right…

Sigh… you know what they say about hindsight, right?

Chapter 21

Assets

The rest of the day was, thankfully, uneventful. I hadn't heard from Tim, which was kind of surprising, but if I'm being honest, I hoped to never hear from him again. It was, at least in part, thanks to him that I had a gun held to my head, not to mention the very real possibility that I might *still* have to move away for my own, and everyone else's, safety.

I also hadn't heard from Anne, which was a little worrying, though not altogether unexpected. She'd just gone through a lot, not to mention finding out a little more about me, like the fact that ghosts are real and that I could sense them, and yet never trusted her enough to reveal that to her about me. Mind you, I'm not entirely certain that she had fully processed this bit of information, though. I think she was still reeling from the reality of the situation. It's not every day you're held at gunpoint *and* knifepoint by a pair of foreign agents.

I wasn't, entirely, sure what to do now, though… Do I act like everything is normal? Do I tackle it head-on? Do I try subtlety? *Could* I do subtlety for something like this?

I just didn't know and it frustrated the *hell* out of me!

I ultimately decided I would go to the store tomorrow morning and kind of… go from there…

I was restless that night, partly from the pain, and partly from worrying about the next day. I eventually gave in and took a painkiller, which dulled the pain, but also made me a bit dizzy. I was lying in a bed that felt like it was slowly spinning… Not pleasant!

Emily agreed to give me a ride to work. We were the first ones there, which was a little alarming. Anne is usually the first one there and the last one to leave.

"Looks like Anne's not here, yet," Emily commented, echoing my own thoughts.

"She might not come in at all…" I lamented, worry heavy in my voice.

"She'll come around," Emily promised unconvincingly.

"Think you can handle having me for a boss?" I asked, arching my brow.

"Sure, why not?" she scoffed, smiling.

"Then I guess it'll just be the two of us…" I sighed.

"And Earl," Emily reminded me.

Oh. Right… I forgot about him… or rather, I had blocked him from my thoughts…

As soon as we got inside and had turned the lights on, we each got a text from Earl telling us to meet him in the bunker.

"So much for normal…" I lamented.

"Come on," Emily chided gently, "it's not like you didn't see this coming!"

I sighed in answer and we made our way downstairs, with Emily, naturally, going first since it took me frickin' *forever* to get down the stairs.

"Stupid cop, stupid broken leg, stupid crutches!" I muttered to myself as I made my way slowly down to the basement.

Earl was there, with the door open, waving us inside.

"What do you *want,* Earl?" I demanded once we were inside the SCIF room proper.

"I want you to play Nightmare," he answered, with a little bit of heat in his voice.

"And me?" Emily asked.

"You'll be getting a new assignment," he informed her. "You'll leave tomorrow morning. Details are here." He handed her a small folder and Emily started perusing the documents while I sat in the folding chair at the table, taking my usual place for these kinds of assignments.

"I assume you got blood from the sensitive?" I asked, looking at the camera on its tripod already set up.

"We did," he confirmed with a nod.

"Okay, so what do you want me to say to him?" I requested, a little huffy that he wasn't already telling me.

"The short answer is that you demand that he cooperates with us, or we'll out him to Prizrak," he explained.

"Out him, how?" I wondered aloud.

"Since we have his blood, he's compromised," Earl continued, sounding ever so slightly annoyed. "If that's not enough, you can tell him that he *might* get to see his brother. Or you can threaten him with nightmares."

"The carrot and the stick?" I scoffed.

"Don't knock it!" he sneered. "It works! Basic psychology."

"Okay, so how will we want him to cooperate?" I asked, wanting specifics.

"You'll direct him to get a burner phone," Earl continued, looking pleased. "He'll give us the number. From there, our people can work with him to set up dead drops with instructions for him. We'll have him doing a misinformation campaign with the odd bit of intelligence inside Prizrak."

"Sounds dangerous for him…" I commented.

"That a problem for you?" he asked, looking mildly suspicious.

"No, I meant he might balk at the idea of putting himself in danger," I defended.

"If he does, then we'll have to bring him in," Earl shrugged, like this was no big deal. "You might have to incapacitate him, though…"

"I don't really have a problem doing that, apart from intentionally *triggering* a flashback…" I sighed. "I mean, the bastard held a gun to my head, not to mention kicking my damned leg, *plus* taking Anne hostage!"

"Good," Earl responded, curtly. "So, you ready?"

"As I'll ever be…" I sighed, not liking this whole situation.

Earl pulled out a small business card with a brown spot on it the color of dried blood. The card was labelled 'Prizrak sensitive' in Earl's blocky writing.

I took the card and, with a small bit of hesitation, pushed a finger onto the dark spot, closed my eyes, and relaxed my mind.

I found myself in a small apartment sitting on one of two beds in the room. I felt tired, like I hadn't slept at *all* that night. The source of the insomnia seemed to be the moans and whimpers of the large man huddled in a corner of the room, not to mention a persistent, throbbing, pain in my arm. The other man seemed to be trying to hide from enemies nobody else could see.

Thoughts came to me, then, all in Russian. Thoughts of what he was going to do now, speculations on who might have done this to his partner, wondering if it might have been Nightmare, and what he should do about it.

There were also thoughts of how he might ambush the girl, again. An image of me in the cast popped up in his head, at that moment, along with speculations that I might be the spooky that had driven the other man mad.

'You'll leave her alone, if you know what's good for you,' I intoned, in Russian, loudly into his head, using a deeper tone than my natural voice. It was my Agent Dreamer voice, but since he had never heard it, I figured it was safer than if I had used my *real* voice.

The man started, violently, jumping to his feet and looking around.

"Where are you?" he demanded aloud, still in Russian.

'I could be anywhere on the planet!' I sneered.

It took him a stunned moment to make the connection as to who I was.

"Nightmare," he declared in disgust.

'Yes,' I confirmed. *'We have your blood. You belong to me now!'*

Yes, I know this is a bit cliché, but people *expect* clichés! The closer I could fit his script of what to expect, the smoother this talk would go.

"What do you want?" he hissed, trying to think of a way out of this mess.

'First, stop trying to find a way out of your situation,' I demanded. *'I know your thoughts. You are trapped.'*

The man stopped, collected his thoughts as he took in what I had just told him, and took several deep breaths to calm himself.

'It might be easier if we communicated like this,' he thought.

'Good!' I encouraged. *'Now you're catching on!'*

'So, I am compromised,' he lamented. *'Does Prizrak know, yet?'*

'We haven't told them,' I assured him. *'We have no reason to… yet.'*

'Yes, I figured as much,' he sighed. *'So, you want me to spy on Prizrak for you?'*

'That might be too dangerous,' I cautioned. *'We'd rather not lose you, just yet. Not after all the trouble we went through to get you in the first place.'*

'So, disinformation then,' he stated, rather than asked. *'Maybe I pretend I have lead on Nightmare…'*

'Good idea!' I encouraged with a smile on my face.

'Why should I help you?' he asked, sounding a little perfunctory, like he just wanted to know all his options.

'Isn't being compromised with Prizrak enough?' I asked, skeptically.

'They don't know, yet,' he shrugged. *'Why should you tell them?'*

'To get your cooperation,' I answered, not seeing where he was going with this.

'Assuming they believe you,' he postulated, feeling a little doubtful at this, *'then they take me off crucial assignments.'*

'They might also kill you,' I retorted.

'Possible, but not likely,' he smirked. *'I am too valuable to them. I know when broadcaster is using their ability. This is rare ability and highly useful!'*

'But not when a sensitive is in your head,' I countered.

'True,' he nodded. *'Is still not enough.'*

'Then I have two options for you,' I sighed. *'The carrot and the stick. Which would you prefer?'*

'What sort of carrot?' he asked, feeling slightly hopeful.

'Work with us enough and you'll see your brother,' I answered.

A flush of surprise and hope bloomed within him, only to be mercilessly hammered down.

'And the stick?' he asked, more for form's sake.

For answer, I showed him a few *select* images and sensations from Betty Tightwad's death. I took it as far as I dared without triggering a *full* flashback.

'Enough!' he shouted into my head. *'I get point! Nightmare is good name for you!'*

'So, will you cooperate?' I asked, feeling close to sealing the deal.

'Yes,' he agreed. *'I will go buy burner phone. You will watch and see the phone number. Your people can contact me on that.'*

'It's nice working with a pro,' I purred into his head, making him smile at the compliment.

'But first,' he declared, standing up and pulling his gun, *'I need to take care of something.'*

With that, he shot his partner in the head! The shot was loud enough that I worried somebody might hear, and he'd be arrested before he could be of any use to us!

'What are you doing?' I demanded harshly.

'He was liability,' he shrugged. *'Where I come from, you put mad dogs down.'*

I confess I was too stunned to say anything else, so I left him to his work. His thoughts focused on the story he would tell Prizrak.

'Blame it on Nightmare,' I suggested a little hesitantly.

'Yes,' he agreed, liking the idea. *'Nightmare got into his head, compromising him. Must have driven him insane. He became liability, so I put him down.'*

The agent stripped his former comrade of his identification and weapons before shoving them into a bag and leaving the room at a casual pace. I didn't hear any signs of panic or people rushing to see what that loud noise was, so I guessed the place was either vacant, abandoned, or he had paid off enough people to look the other way.

In the end, it all amounts to the same, I guess…

I saw him get into his car, drive to the nearest electronics store, and buy a cheap cell phone with cash. I relayed the number to Earl and told the agent that we would be in contact soon. He nodded at this and I disconnected.

"What about the man's partner?" Earl asked me after I set the card down.

"He shot him," I answered, still slightly in shock, but not as much as I *thought* I'd be. After all, I had just seen a man casually *kill* his partner over something *I* had done to him!

The agent may have killed him, but I was the one responsible…

Earl eyed me suspiciously, perhaps trying to gauge the truth of what I had just said.

"The other man, the hitman…" I continued, suddenly feeling the weight of what I had done and seen starting to crush me. "What I did to him… the ghosts… they drove him mad…"

I confess I was trembling by this point, the enormity finally hitting me.

"So the sensitive put him down like a dog," Emily finished for me, reminding me that she was still there.

"That's what he said, almost word-for-word..." I gasped.

"Jane..." Earl cajoled, his voice somewhere between stern and compassionate. "You didn't kill him."

"But he died because of what I did to him!" I shot back heatedly.

"Why do you care?" Emily asked, somewhat snidely. "He was a hitman, wasn't he? He held a *knife* to Anne's *throat!* I say good riddance!"

"Maybe..." I conceded, still feeling like shit.

"Jane, if he hadn't done it, I would have ordered you to make him do it," Earl declared, sternly. "The other man was too much of a liability to be allowed to live."

I nodded, mutely, at this. I could see the cold, hard, logic of it, but it all seemed so damned *heartless* to me. *This* is one of the reasons I hated working for the CIA. I *vastly* preferred my work with project Top Hat because the line between good and evil was crystal clear. Save the victim so that the perpetrator can be prosecuted.

Simple. Clean. *Clear.*

This, though... this was anything *but* clear...

"So, how's he going to explain his dead partner to his people?" Emily asked, bluntly.

"I told him to blame Nightmare..." I waved off. "He was concocting a story that Nightmare had compromised him, made him go mad, which forced the agent to cut their losses. He seemed confident he could sell it."

"Good," Earl nodded approvingly.

"Earl?" I asked with a lump in my throat after a long moment of collecting my thoughts. "Am I safe, now?"

"As safe as we can make it," Earl sighed, perhaps sensing how vulnerable I was feeling. "Tim won't be bothering you again, if he knows what's good for him. He'll be another part of our disinformation campaign. I've got his card for you. Feel free to spy on him as much as you want."

I nodded weakly at this, even as I numbly accepted the little business card with another brown stain on it and Tim's name written in Earl's hand.

I had a hard time resisting the urge to pull out Mr. Fluffybutt and hug him tightly. I wanted to *cling* to my little bunny life preserver and just pretend that *none* of this had happened. That everything was gonna be *okay* and that Anne would come in and be her usual *cheery* self and we would *laugh* about what a silly *dream* this had been!

I wanted someone to tell me this wasn't real.

Dammit, I was almost *twenty years old!* I've been living on my *own* for *years* now! I'm an *adult,* dammit!

So why don't I feel like one?

Chapter 22

Goodbyes

Anne didn't come in that day… or the next… or the day after…

I tried texting her, but got no reply. Once, I even screwed up my courage to call her directly, but only got her voicemail…

So, it was just me trying to run the store and I confess that I was running myself ragged. I was basically working *two* full-time jobs, one of which drained me to the point of exhaustion, while the other needed me to stay awake and deal with customers, which is *not* an easy thing to do when you're running on not-enough sleep and a shortened temper!

It was over a week before Anne came back into the store… When I saw her walk through the front door, I confess I was thrilled beyond measure to see her again!

Anne, though, was *not* thrilled…

"You're leaving, aren't you?" I nearly sobbed when I saw her face and realized what was coming. I had half-expected this, but even so, the *reality* of it hits a helluva lot harder than the *theory* of it.

"You reading my mind?" she asked, half-serious.

"Just your face," I confessed. "I kinda saw this coming, given what you went through…"

"How can you *stand* it?" she demanded, anger in her voice. "Two men came in here and held a *gun* to my face, then one took a *knife* to my throat! *You* had a *gun* at your *head!*"

"It's not the first time someone has held a gun on me," I told her, glancing down at my cast and remembering the bullet that had shattered one of my leg bones. "Besides, I've got a therapist that I see regularly… I could give you his name! But… he might be pricey… plus he's in New York…" I mumbled at the end.

Anne gave me one of those 'are you serious?' looks and my suggestions died in my throat.

"You should leave, too!" Anne suggested.

"I *can't!*" I whined.

"Why the hell *not?*" she demanded, heatedly.

"I have people here that count on me…" I confessed.

"Like who? *Earl?* Screw him!" Anne almost screamed.

"Not *just* Earl!" I shot back. "People that can't leave… If I left, they'd make trouble… trouble that wasn't their fault…"

Anne gave me an inscrutable look and I wanted to reach out to her to *know* what she was thinking, but I restrained myself… *barely.*

"Ghosts…" I whispered after the pause was getting awkward. "I live with a couple of ghosts, okay? They're wonderful kids and if I left, they'd be *furious* because they'd feel so *betrayed!* And, you know what? They'd be *right* to feel betrayed!"

I confess I was holding back tears as I told her this.

"Can't you, I dunno… help them move on or something?" she asked after a moment. I think she was still trying to come to grips with the idea that ghosts are real and that I really *did* live in a haunted mansion and that I was *friends* with them!

"I've *tried*," I lamented. "They like me and they want to protect me. Besides…" I sighed, screwing up my courage to confess the realization I had come to grips with, "this is the *first* place that has *ever* felt like a *home* to me! I can't just *abandon* it when things get rough!"

Anne looked hurt at the implied accusation and I regretted it immediately.

"No, wait!" I gasped. "I didn't mean it like that!"

"It's okay, Jane…" Anne interrupted, holding up a hand. "Beth was right, you know… you really *are* fearless!"

"No, I'm not!" I pleaded. "I'm just better at *hiding* it!"

"Maybe," she shrugged, clearly not convinced.

"So… what are you going to do now?" I asked, a lump in my throat.

"I've just mailed my resignation in to 'corporate' and now…" she answered, slowly. "Now, I think I'm going to retire. My husband and I have talked it over and… I just can't stay here…"

"Where will you go?" I asked, fighting damned hard to keep from breaking down. Dammit, it wasn't fair! I had risked my life to keep from losing her! I had saved her *life*, but she was still *leaving!* I was gonna lose her *anyway!*

"We were thinking south…" Anne admitted. "Maybe someplace it doesn't snow… That's always been our dream, anyway… Now seems like a good time to make it happen, what with the nightmares…"

"Nightmares?" I choked. "You have… nightmares over it?"

"Every night," she confessed.

"Anne, I'm *so* sorry! I never meant…" I was practically sobbing at this point.

"It's okay, Jane!" she interrupted again, cutting me off with a hand gesture. "It's not your fault. I don't blame you."

I wanted to scream that it *was* my fault and to *beg* her to stay, but… I had no right. It was her decision, not mine. Besides, if she stayed, and was miserable, that would be *entirely* my fault. Anne didn't have the resources I did for dealing with trauma like that. I couldn't blame her for not wanting to be someplace that was nothing but triggers for her. After all, if I was in her position, I'd probably do the same thing!

"Then I wish you well!" I smiled through the tears. "May you find peace in your journey."

"Thank you," she answered, gratefully. "Hey, look at the bright side, maybe 'corporate' will make you the manager, now!"

"Yeah, probably!" I agreed, giving a weak chuckle around the lump in my throat.

Anne looked like she was wavering between running to me and just leaving. I could see the concern on her face. I think she was worried that if she hugged me, or something, that I'd pick up on whatever thoughts she was having. Hell and blast, knowing her, she probably didn't want to burden me with her fears and worries!

"It gets better," I told her after a long moment. "It never, *quite*, goes away, but you get better at dealing with it. It goes from a sharp, constant, pain to a dull ache, with only the odd bit of fresh stabbing…"

"You sound like an expert!" she chuckled, halfheartedly.

"Lot of trauma…" I confessed quietly. "It's harder to wound scar tissue…"

Anne looked troubled, just then, like she was seeing me in a new light. I think she'd always known that I was troubled, but she never quite realized just how bad it was.

"People are stronger than they think," I shrugged, trying to ignore her concern. "You do what you have to, to survive. There's no shame in that, or in seeking help. Remember, it takes a special kind of courage to ask for help. I don't ever want you to feel afraid of asking me for help. If you *ever* need my help, or just want to talk to me, I'm here for you. Anytime, day or night, I'll help you, if I can. And if I can't, I'll find someone who *can* help you, okay?"

Anne nodded, tears threatening to spill over. She was still afraid of coming closer to me, which I tried not to take personally.

"I will. Thank you," she finally stammered before turning on her heel and leaving the store that had once been hers, for the last time.

It would be *years* before I would see her again, and then only because she was in dire need of help and she didn't know who else to turn to for something so bizarre. I'd sometimes get postcards from her, which I treasured, and the odd email or text, but like most people separated by distance, we drifted apart. There's nothing good or bad with drifting apart, it's just a fact of life, like the rising of the tide.

I confess I was still somewhat of a wreck when Beth came into the store, looking eager to spread some gossip, and perhaps scenting some on me. Today, her color was a bright peach, from her shoes, to her knee-length skirt, to her top and jacket, and even her purse! All were the same shade of peach, which often made me wonder if she didn't make her own clothes, or something, in order to get such a perfect match on the colors.

"Jane!" she called, cheerfully. *"There* you are!"

"Here I am!" I agreed, mentally preparing myself to be ready to say no to anything she might have planned for me.

"I just heard that Anne was *retiring!"* she told me, sounding shocked.

"Yeah…" I agreed with a mournful sigh. "I think the attempted robbery pushed her to it…" I added, reinforcing the lie we had been telling.

"I thought as much!" she nodded, knowingly. "I heard *you* were a *hero,* though!"

"No, I really *wasn't!*" I protested. "I just ducked when things started going wrong!"

"Nonsense!" she chided, sternly. "The no-good thieves didn't get away with *anything* and I'm *certain* you were the reason for that! Fearless Jane! That's what I'll call you from now on!"

"Please don't." I begged, to no avail, sadly.

"By the way…" she transitioned, slyly. "What's going on with you and Tim? I thought this would be the *perfect* time to get you two back together again, but when I brought it up, he just got this terrified look in his eyes! What did you *do* to him, anyway?"

"Well…" I paused, biting my lip, trying to think up a good lie on the spot. "I kind-of threatened him with… *libel* when he wouldn't leave me alone…"

"Libel?" Beth gasped in surprise, with just the faintest hint of eagerness, like she was scenting blood in the water. "That's a *serious* charge! But…" she paused, a finger to her lips. "I don't recall him writing anything about you…"

I shrugged at this and continued my lie, "I figured with how much he writes on that blog of his, and given my reputation around town, that he must have written *something* about me. Judging by the way he reacted…" I left off, letting her finish the rest.

Beth nodded at this, looking like she was ready to start searching through everything Tim had written, both in the local paper and online, to see what might have spooked him like that.

I confess that the thought of Beth spending so much time researching a lie I had made up on the spot was oddly satisfying to me. The more time she spent on *that,* the less time she'd spend gossiping about *me!* I've had *more* than enough trouble with gossips, thank you very much!

"Well, I think you can do better than *him,* then!" Beth declared, a sly look on her face that sent klaxons blaring in my head!

"Beth…" I warned, "what are you thinking?"

"Well, I was thinking that the new deputy…" she started, her look going from sly to coy.

"John Hart?" I asked, my heart jumping to my throat!

"That's the one!" she smiled, like the wolf that had just sighted a rabbit caught in a trap.

"What… what about him?" I asked, going for nonchalant, and failing miserably.

"Well, I heard he's single!" she answered, arching her eyebrows several times in encouragement.

"You know, I heard that, too…" I purred. "But… do you think he'd be interested in me? I mean…" I looked down at myself and saw only plainness, with nothing especially *special* about me, at least, nothing I could share with him, since, you know, *classified,* but Beth didn't need to know that!

"Oh, you'd be surprised, dear!" she chuckled. "Don't you know that guys often like the plain girls that are more down-to-earth and *honest?* I'm sure he'd like you *fine!"*

Honest, *right…*

"Really?" I asked, a little giddily.

"I'll tell you what," she smirked, "I'll set the whole thing up for the two of you!"

"Thank you, Beth, I really appreciate it!" I told her, for once completely sincere.

Unfortunately, due to scheduling conflicts, not to mention my utter exhaustion at managing what amounted to *two* full-time jobs, it would be *months* before John and I had our first date, which would only be my second date in my life. To say that the date ended in disaster would be an understatement, but to say that it was a *bad* date, would be somewhat misleading.

But the tale of our first date is a story for another time…